Robert Sadler

Empty in the End

All characters, names, locations
and events in this novel are used
in a fictional manner.

Bahamut Publishing
ISBN: 978-0615821450

Follow the book online at
EmptyintheEnd.com &
Facebook.com/EmptyintheEnd

This novel is dedicated to everyone
who reads even a single word of it.

Thank you.

Prologue

The fear of death follows from the fear of life. A man who lives fully is prepared to die at any time. – Mark Twain.

That's an awfully deep message to be written with lipstick in a bathroom stall, Miranda thought. At least it was better than the multitude of other vulgar writings lining the wall. Scanning it informed her that dozens of people had been there, even more were in love and twice as many as that left their phone numbers in case the reader was looking for a good time. *I should have just peed at the office.*

She was in the bathroom of a disgusting bar that she wouldn't have stepped foot into had she not been about to piss herself. The tiles were yellow, but she was sure they were supposed to be white. More of the wall was covered with marker than not, and every porcelain fixture she saw since entering was cracked. The bar was a smoke-filled dive visited only by depressed alcoholics with nowhere else to go. It showed years of abuse and neglect, and would have failed miserably in any other part of the city. Then again, every business in the Orange District would have failed outside of it.

The standards there were subpar, to put it nicely. She would know, she spent more than nine hours a day trying to clean it up.

Miranda worked in the heart of the Orange District at a youth center she had established with the money from her wealthy father's will. She didn't feel she had any more right to the inheritance than anyone else, so she decided to share it. Working at the center was an uphill battle if ever there was one, but it gave her a sense of accomplishment that no desk job ever would. She helped the world, or at least she liked to think she did. Sometimes she wasn't so sure. Many days were painful. She'd seen kids come in just minutes after being beaten ruthlessly by their parents. She'd been begged by loving but poor parents to let their children spend the night in the warm building. Every day brought new horrors, but it was her job to provide hope to the sufferers and she wouldn't have traded the responsibility for the world.

That evening she stayed late to help a ten-year-old Hispanic boy named Vincent with his homework. He was a shining example that beautiful things could come from the filthiest of places. He was intelligent, polite and creative despite being born to two crack-heads who couldn't care less about his well-being. It wasn't rare for Miranda to become a parental figure to the children who attended the center. It was what made it all worth it. Kids like that needed an adult they could love instead of fear. It was her goal to be just that. She hated the idea of them growing up thinking that childhoods were meant to be as painful as theirs.

After finishing with Vincent, she closed up and drove him home. He normally walked the mile or so to his apartment, but they left later than normal and she didn't feel right about letting him make the trek in the dark. She needed to use the bathroom before leaving, but didn't want to keep Vincent waiting, and convinced herself that she could hold it. She was wrong. After dropping him off, her situation became desperate, leading her to the hole-in-the-wall she was currently sitting in. Husky Harry's was the name. It was a dumb name, and she thought so every day when she drove by it on the way to work. She never thought she'd actually step foot in the place.

She was wiping herself when she heard a loud bang emanate from somewhere in the bar. It startled her, causing the sheet of toilet paper to fall from her hand. It sounded like a gunshot, though she wasn't sure she'd ever heard one in person. For all she knew, it was just a car backfiring. A very loud car. She went about her business assuming it was nothing. Miranda wasn't one to panic without a very good reason to. She struggled in the tiny stall to get up and pull herself together, then washed her hands. As she dried them she heard another bang, followed by a short silence and three more. It was strange – out of this group of four, the first, third and fourth were far quieter than the original she had heard moments ago. The second, however, was softer than the original, but louder than the others.

She started to worry now. A bang was one thing, but five of them spaced out like that at various volumes in a neighborhood like this meant violence. Certainty replaced doubt. These *were* gunshots, and they were coming from different shooters. She tiptoed over to the door and cracked it open to peek out. As she touched the handle, a sixth and seventh shot rang out. These two were distant.

Jesus Christ! What the hell is going on? A slight pause led to an eighth and ninth. She opened the door slowly and glanced out. The bar was completely empty. Something had definitely happened here – and whatever it was, the patrons didn't want to stick around for it. She was confident that the action had moved outside, but she still waited a minute or two for more shots. When none came, she slipped out of the bathroom. Nothing in the bar seemed out of place except for the fact that it was abandoned. She pulled out her phone and dialed 9-1-1.

"9-1-1, where is your emergency?" an operator asked.

"Um, it's Husky Harry's. I'm not sure of the address, but it's a bar in the Orange District." Miranda continued to investigate as she talked.

"OK, we've already received a call on the matter and the police have been dispatched. Are you in any present danger?"

"No, I don't think so." She hoped the thought was correct.

"Could you please tell me what you saw."

"I didn't see anything but I heard gunshots while I was in the bathroom here. I came out and no one was left in the bar. I'm not sure what happened, but there was definitely a lot of shooting."

"How many shots did you hear ma'am?"

Miranda struggled to remember exactly. "Uh, either eight or nine. Nine I think."

"OK. Like I said, officers are on their way. Their ETA is about four minutes."

"Thank you," Miranda said and hung up before getting a response.

Her attention was drawn to the back of the bar, where an open door to a small room begged to be investigated. Somehow it looked out of place, but what really caught her eye was what appeared to be blood on the back wall. It was pretty far from her and through a doorway, but she felt strongly enough about her observation to get a closer look. She strode by a cluster of pool tables and approached the door. There was a sign above it identifying it as "The Rain Room," whatever that meant. As she closed in on the room, she was petrified by what was inside.

On the floor was a young man and woman, both dead and covered in so much blood that Miranda couldn't tell where it had come from. The man sat on the floor with his back against a couch and a gun in his hand, while the woman lay in his lap. Was it a murder-suicide? That's how it looked. Her mind recalled all of those terrible news stories of husbands murdering their wives and then cowardly turning the gun on themselves. That scenario couldn't have accounted for all the shots she heard, though. There were at least eight of them, probably nine. The later ones couldn't have come from inside the bar.

This isn't right.

She felt queasy. In her thirty-nine years on this planet, she only saw one dead body – her father's. Somehow she had avoided wakes and funerals until his. On top of that, she hated the sight of blood. It made her stomach rebel. She threw up on the floor of the room, feet away from the bodies. Her head was spinning along with her stomach. She needed to get out of there. The walls were closing in.

Fresh air. I need fresh air. She stumbled out of the room clumsily, finding it difficult to focus. The image of the dead clouded that of her surroundings. To her right she saw a fire exit sign and moved towards it. She pushed the back door open and inhaled the fresh, crisp air of the alleyway. It tasted like freedom.

She was terribly happy to be out of there, but her relief was short-lived. As she turned the corner to her left, she was confronted by two more bodies on the ground.

More? What happened here? This pair was even worse than the last, surrounded by an even more shocking amount of blood.

She had never seen so much, didn't think two humans could even hold it all. They were a male and female – just like the other two – and were both face-down on the concrete. She didn't see a wound on the man, but the woman had three holes in the back of her shirt.

Did the man inside with the gun do this? How could he? He would have had to kill these two, then return inside and kill the girl and himself. No, that's wrong. It doesn't explain why the first and third shots were louder than the rest.

Miranda couldn't think about it, her head wasn't bothering with logistics now. Either way, four people had been brutally killed. Every ounce of her said to run as fast and as far away as she could.

She saw the street at the end of the alley. Cars passed, oblivious to the fact that they were driving by a horrific crime scene. The street was her goal. Everything would be alright if she could make it there. Something else caught her eye as her plan was decided. About twenty yards away, between her and her destination, was yet another body. She was further devastated when she realized that it had the shape of a child. It was too far away to make out any wounds, though she assumed if she went closer she would discover a bullet hole. As if that wasn't enough, her eye moved past the poor thing and spotted a sixth corpse at the very end of the alley.

She threw up again, dropping to her knees in weakness. *Six bodies. This is a massacre.* She felt like she was in a horror movie. She wiped off her mouth and turned in the opposite direction. Her heart raced, causing physical pain. Every beat was a stab to her chest. She stumbled past the two victims in the blood puddle and rounded the corner where she had come from. The stabs grew worse as she looked down at the bloody figures and the gruesome spectacle they created. The alley had another exit ahead. She hoped to God there would be no more discoveries. One more would be the death of her.

Five steps past the corner, her legs gave up. She fell to the ground, clutching her chest in agony. She'd never had a heart attack – she was thirty-nine and healthy – but she was positive she was having one now. She rolled over onto her back and focused on breathing normally. She tried to yell, but nothing came out. The only outcome was a more furious pain. She closed her eyes, accepting her powerlessness. She only hoped the police and paramedics would arrive before it was too late.

"An Interview with Arthur Candle"
Red Herring Mystery Magazine, October 2023

New Englanders over the age of twenty-five are sure to re-member the mysterious Double-H Massacre that rocked the city of Canterville fifteen years ago. To this day, the details of the events that took place in a small, unsuspecting bar called Husky Harry's are unknown. Six lives were lost within a mat-ter of minutes, with two more deaths strangely connected to the event. The debates and theories rage on as followers of the case continue their attempts to work out the puzzle. With the anniversary of the unsolved bloodbath just a week away, *Red Herring* sat down with Detective Arthur Candle, the lead detective in the now closed investigation.

RED HERRING: Thank you for joining us, Detective Can-dle. Could you start by telling us why you think the Double-H Massacre continues to hold the interest of unsolved mystery aficionados after all these years?

ARTHUR CANDLE: Thanks for having me. Well, it has all the components of a great mystery. It's still unsolved, for one. It was brutal, it was strange. I think, however, the most striking reason for the ongoing interest in the case is that the victims and their causes of death simply don't make much sense. Five victims suffered from gunshot wounds, one of which was self-inflicted. One victim had his throat cut and another died without any physical wounds whatsoever. The victims themselves were a motley group, ranging from a pimp to an 11-year-old narcoleptic boy. On top of that, we know there is an unidentified suspect somewhere out there that had a hand in what went down. This all made a perfect melting pot for theories and myths to be born. Shit, I'm surprised there hasn't been a movie made yet. Oh, sorry... can I say "shit"?

RH: Feel free to use any language you'd like. *Red Herring* is an uncensored publication for adults. We suspect your account of the case will involve worse than that.

AC: Oh, yes. Much worse.

RH: Can you walk our readers through your inspection of the crime scene that night?

AC: Sure, sure. It was a Friday evening when I got the call. I showed up to [Husky Harry's] and was informed by another officer, Casey O'Doyle, that there were seven people dead, in and around the bar.

RH: Seven people? It was our understanding that there were six fatalities.

AC: Yes, well one of the victims was presumed dead upon my arrival, but ended up surviving, bringing the death toll to six. Since this is a mystery magazine, I'll keep your readers guessing as to who it was. I'm sure those that are familiar with the case already know the details, but for the rest, I'll explain the elements as I discovered them.

RH: You should come work for us. Three questions into the interview and you're already shrouding your answers in secrecy. You'd be perfect for *Red Herring*.

AC: [Laughs] I might just take you up on that offer. Retirement's quite boring for an old bastard like me who spent his life tracking down criminals. [Laughs again] So anyway, Officer O'Doyle passes me a hand-drawn map of the scene that was done by a rookie. It showed a rough sketch of the building layout, along with the locations of the bodies.

RH: I assume you're referring to the "Darby Sketch?"

AC: Yeah, that's the term the media coined for it. The young rookie that drew it was Officer John Darby. He's the Chief of Police now, wouldn't ya know it? It's funny – me and O'Doyle had a good laugh about it at the scene, teasing him and whatnot, but it ended up helping me take everything in before I even stepped foot into that bar. And, of course, it helped everyone following the case in the media to have a better idea of what happened. Who knew that damn scribble would become famous?

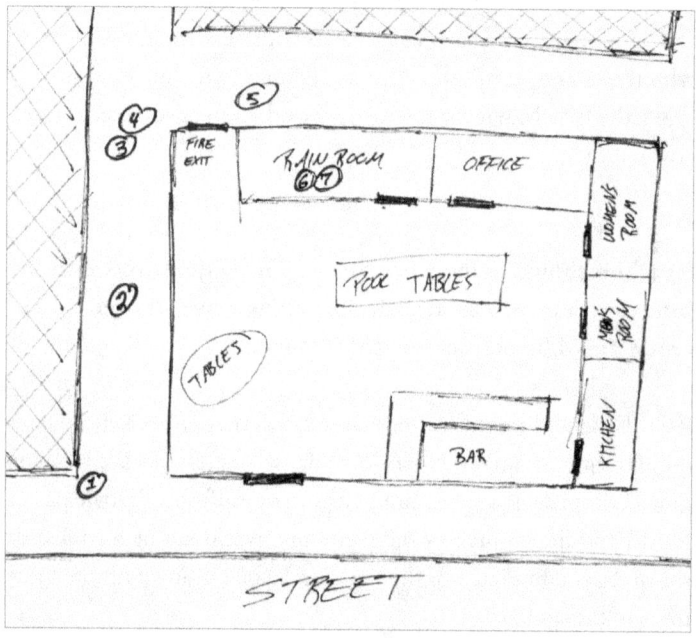

Figure 1 Hand-drawn sketch created by Officer John Darby at the scene of the Double-H Massacre. October 17, 2008.

From the sketch, I saw that there were two bodies inside the bar, both in a room at the rear. The other five were outside the building, in the alleyway. I started my survey inside the bar, since witnesses all claimed that the events started in there.

RH: What were the witnesses' accounts?

AC: The three people present at Husky Harry's who made it out all said the violence started with a gunshot that came from the back of the bar. All three told me they were too busy hightailing it out the front door to get a glimpse of a shooter. We had no description of the suspect besides a hazy recollection that there was a man with an orange shirt in the bar before the shooting started.

Once they were out, they all heard more shots outside, in the alley beside the building. Other people in the area corroborated this. All recalled hearing between 7 and 10 shots total. We know there were at least 7, which is the number that found their way into the victims.

RH: And what did you find upon examining the bodies?

AC: I found a friggin' mess, that's what! [Chuckles, then sighs] I can joke about it now, but trust me when I tell you that it was a struggle to not run out of that place. It was bad. Like I said, I started inside the bar, which brought me to young man named Jacob Driscoll and a girl in her twenties who had no identification.

RH: And they were found in the Rain Room, correct? There's been a lot of speculation about that room since, as I understand.

AC: Yes, they were in the Rain Room, which *has* had a lot of controversy around it. More on that later, I'm sure. These two were numbers 6 and 7 in the Darby Sketch. Both of them were on the floor. Jacob Driscoll was sitting up with his back against the base of a couch, and the blonde female with him was laying on his lap. Driscoll was dead from what was clearly a self-inflicted gunshot wound to the head. The female had been shot in the stomach. It wasn't clear at the time whether Driscoll was responsible for her death, or any of the others. I've investigated more than enough murder-suicides in my day, and that was my initial impression.

From there, I exited the building through the rear and saw 39-year-old Miranda Allen on her back in the alleyway. She's number 5. There wasn't a scratch on her; nothing to indicate her cause of death. When I found her, she still had her eyes open. Still looked like she was in pain. I actually knew of her from some community events. Good person. She inherited $23 million from her deceased father and went right to work putting it into the community. Can't say that I'd do the same.

RH: Nor can I. What were your thoughts at the time about her cause of death, since there was no physical damage to her?

AC: Truth be told, I didn't know what to think. Maybe a heart attack. I'll tell you one thing though, seeing her there made me realize that this wasn't going to be no run-of-the-mill investigation. Of course it didn't get any better with the next two bodies.

RH: You're referring to 3 and 4?

AC: I am. Those two were especially grisly. Number 4 was Phil Harris, the owner of the bar. He was face-down in a pool of blood. Closer examination revealed that his throat had been cut. Number 3 was an unidentified black female in her early twenties. She had three gunshot wounds in her torso. She was holding a Swiss army knife, which was presumably used to kill Phil Harris. To this day, we don't know why.

RH: So things were really getting strange at this point?

AC: Absolutely. We had an apparent murder-suicide inside the bar, and what looked like a completely separate slashing and shooting outside. Plus a victim without any wounds thrown in the mix. The three events seemed unrelated, but that would make even less sense than if they were connected.

RH: And there were still two more to go.

AC: Yes, the next victim was a young boy, number 2 on the sketch. That one hit me hard. It still makes my eyes water when I think about him. The poor thing was face-down with a bullet hole in the back of his head. It was clear he was running when he got shot, maybe away from whatever was going on with Phil Harris and the female with the knife. It's chilling to think of the terror he must have felt before being hit. I wanted the person responsible to die, if they weren't already among the bodies scattered throughout the place.

RH: Are those kinds of feelings common among officers and detectives?

AC: Common? No. But they certainly come up. When you investigate as many cases as my colleagues and I have, you see the worst kinds of people. Animals without a shred of conscience. So, yeah … seeing that kid laying there hurt. Hurt real bad.

He was wearing a backpack that was stocked like he'd made a long trip. There was food and drinks in there; a flashlight. The kind of stuff a kid would think he needed for a journey. There was no real identification in there, but there *was* a letter that referred to him as "Gabriel." It was addressed to a Mr. and Mrs. Morrison, who we rightly assumed were his parents. They were the first people I called afterward.

The last person I found at the scene was number 1. We knew who he was. Piece of shit named Ron Toomey. He was a pimp, and not small-time, either. Half the fucking prostitution in the area came from his girls – excuse my language. Can't say I was too banged up about finding him dead with a bullet in his face. He had a gun in his hand, but the clip was full; he didn't shoot anything.

RH: Being faced with such bizarre evidence must have been intimidating.

AC: It was quite the puzzle. So much so that we still don't know everything that happened.

RH: Even with many details still a mystery, the investigation *did* uncover a lot of baffling information about the victims and what led them to Husky Harry's that night. Could you go over what we now know about these individuals?

5

IRE
EXIT

RAIN BOOM

6 7

POOL T

TABLES

Jake's Issue

"Fine you junkie bitch, don't open the door," Jake yelled, his mouth a millimeter from the cracked white paint of the door. "Just sit in there and stick another shot of fake bliss into your fucking arm!"

He regretted saying it the second it leaped from his lips, but he wasn't about to take it back. He was far too deep into a rage to have control over that. Every muscle in his body was tense. He was standing in the hallway attracting the attention of everyone in the apartment building and not giving a fuck. Later, he would give a fuck. Right now, however, his attitude was pure apathy toward anything besides him and his enemy on the other side of that door.

"I'm not doping, you asshole, I just don't wanna talk to you," Faith said back, strangely subdued. Then, as if realizing that there wasn't enough fire in her last statement, she yelled, "And if you ever call me a junkie bitch again I'll cut your fucking balls off and feed them to you! Now get the fuck out of here before one of my neighbors calls the cops!"

Bang!

Jake wailed on the door with the strongest punch he could

muster. It was violent enough to add a few red dots to the plethora of stains littering the hall. He left with a look in his eyes that would have kept even the hardest onlooker out of his way. The path exiting the building was an obstacle course of trash, everything from old bicycles to a torn up recliner. He charged through the rubbish like it didn't exist.

He stormed out of the building into the parking lot and was met with a disgusted look from one of Faith's neighbors. This wasn't the first time they had caused a scene here. Their fights weren't rare by any means. No doubt the neighbors were familiar with their voices, whether they had ever seen them or not. Jake endured many post-battle walks of shame. Disgruntled neighbors always seemed to be there to hit him with their disapproving gazes.

He jumped through the open window of his Pontiac, not at all smoothly because of his state of mind. Its door handle had been torn off three months ago when Faith borrowed it for a night and somehow grazed a parking meter. That stunt had left him with a shiny new car that was in perfect condition besides a dysfunctional door. His parents – who had bought him the car – used it as yet another example of why he should avoid Faith at all costs. It was impossible to hide her problems from them. They knew and they hated the relationship.

Jake stabbed the car with his key and took off from The Swan Orchard Apartments.

An hour ago, Jake and Faith were getting ready to go out for a quiet dinner. Then, he somehow ended up standing outside of her apartment in a filthy hallway that hadn't been cleaned in years yelling like a maniac. Now he was on the highway, pissed off and starving.

That's it, I'm done with this, he thought as dozens of Faith's ridiculous acts of stupidity zipped through is mind. Getting arrested for assaulting a woman in a Walmart. Crashing a friend's Mercedes while high on heroin. Then there was the real doozy: cheating on him and getting pregnant. That "mistake" as she called it, ended their relationship for two years, during which the child was removed from her custody because of her drug use. Jake was ashamed that he even allowed their relationship to resume after those two years. That should have been his ticket to freedom. He knew very well that his continued involvement with her bullshit was above and beyond the foolishness of any of her offenses.

If he had stumbled upon Faith in the last few years, he would have dismissed her as a delinquent and strolled on by. Her beauty was hidden by sunken eyes and cheeks, her vitality replaced with a constant look of weakness. Unfortunately for him, she had attached herself to his life when they were both eight years old. That was the only reason he felt he owed her loyalty. He was aware that he could vastly improve his situation by throwing that loyalty away. A twenty year relationship isn't something that is easily tossed aside, however. For half of those twenty tumultuous years, their relationship had been romantic, if you could consider their current situation romantic. And so he was also aware that their codependency would live on. He loved her, after all, and nothing she could do would dispel that.

Who am I kidding? I'm not even close to done with this shit. Fuck.

A short time later – and after brooding and dwelling on many more acts of stupidity – Jake pulled into parking spot twenty-three of The Parted Meadow Apartment Community. His own home was far from the dump that Faith was stuck living in. Unlike her, he was responsible and able to live in a modest but comfortable apartment. He had been working brutal shifts as a bartender while fighting his way through law school, an opportunity he had his parents to thank for.

Jake benefitted from being an only child in an upper-middle class family. His childhood was mostly a happy one. His parents owned a successful pharmacy, so money was never a problem. They loved each other and they loved him. He was given everything he needed physically and emotionally, never taking it for granted. He was constantly aware of his own good fortune, mostly because of its stark contrast to Faith's. He wished she had known the same kind of childhood.

Jake's family wasn't without its problems, though. His mother had been a manic depressive for as long as he could re-member, which brought strain to the family but never tore it apart. Sometimes he thought it had actually strengthened it, terrible and agonizing as it was. He remembered watching her fill with energy, ready to take on the world. It was exhilarating when he was a child but worrisome later in life. These flashes of productivity and joy were inevitably followed by days of little to no speech. He would try talking to her as she sat in her dimly lit bedroom, her mind miles from the outside world. Her responses were always limited to two words at a time. To this day his mood dropped when he thought of it.

Once inside his apartment, Jake headed straight to the kitchen to brew a pot of his favorite stress reliever. Convinced that he needed to occupy his mind to get its focus off of Faith, he cracked open a textbook. He was taking the bar exam in two weeks and couldn't afford to be distracted by childish shit, which was exactly what his fight with Faith was.

I'm saturated with debt and rapidly approaching the last roadblock between me and the means to pay it. I should have my shit together. My life shouldn't be split between a responsible adulthood and a foolish childhood.

Less than a minute later, he knew studying for his future was futile. He tossed the textbook aside. He sat back on the couch and stared at the ceiling, wondering what the hell he was doing with himself. It was a common thought that bounced around in his head, despite not being welcome. In fact, Jake's biggest problem was unwelcome thoughts burdening him with their presence. Perhaps his second biggest problem.

The life of the introvert, he thought. *Your best friend and your worst enemy rolled into one nagging creature trapped inside your head making you confident and self-loathing at the same time. Woe is me.*

He snapped out of his daze and headed back into the kitchen to see how the coffee was progressing. The pot was still brewing and half empty, but he poured himself a cup anyway, which made for a strong taste. He opened the cabinet where he kept the snacks and grabbed a few cookies to munch on. He was starving, since his dinner plans had been thrown out the window the second he realized Faith was high. He hadn't gone food shopping in about ten days, so cookies were his best option.

His phone rang before he could finish the first one. He took a look at the screen, knowing damn well who it was going to be.

Sure enough, Faith's smiling photograph was shown with a large, green "Answer" button below it. He let it ring with no intention of hearing her out. He was just beginning to calm his nerves and answering her call would reverse that progress.

He couldn't help staring at the photo on the screen. It had been taken nine years earlier during a visit to the beach. It reminded him of a life without stress. This was before everything went downhill. Faith was beaming and drug-free. He had his suspicions that she had been dabbling at the time, but it was a far cry from what she'd since become. Anyone looking at the photo would have seen a gorgeous blonde girl who was clearly enjoying herself. Enjoying life. She was nineteen, radiant, perfect in height and weight. He used to think he was the luckiest guy on the planet to have hooked a goddess like her. Now he wished he could unhook her.

The only smidgen of ugliness on her entire body had been a great scar that ran from her forehead to just above her right ear. It wasn't the scar itself that was ugly. At the time the photo was taken, she could have had scars all over and her beauty would have still shone through. It was the origin of the scar that was ugly. When she was only seven years old, Faith's father had created it using a straight razor.

Faith had told him the story when they were teenagers, and he wished he could forget it. For the first ten years he knew her, she had lied about how it happened. He didn't remember the phony story, but he did remember the night she told him the truth. They were sixteen and had just started dating. They had gone to a carnival and ended up back at Jake's home, which was then his parents' house. Her high spirits must have gave her the willingness to exorcise her demons, who lived in the true story of that scar. If her father had not already been killed years before in a bar fight,

Jake would have tracked him down and done the job himself. He reserved resentment for her mother as well. He'd only met her a couple times – Faith barely spoke to her – but it was enough to see that she was a weak human being. She would have to be to let that animal harm Faith. A mother was supposed to give her life for her children if need be, but she sat by idly while Faith's childhood was ruined. She certainly deserved a share of the blame.

And so Jake constantly struggled with his anger towards Faith for who she had become. Who was he to judge her? He hadn't grown up in a home with a psychopathic father and a passive mother who did nothing to stop him. And what made her abuse even worse was that she couldn't look into a mirror, see a photo of herself, or even stand beside a pond without being reminded of it.

He knew the odds had been against her from the beginning. His upbringing, while far from perfectly happy, was a big part of why he had turned out to be his current self. Faith was a victim of circumstance. A helpless child unfortunate enough to be born into a world ruled by a savage. That was likely to mold anyone into a drug addict.

Once the phone stopped ringing, a window popped up notifying him of a voicemail message. He knew there would be one. If Faith had called to get something off her chest, then she damn well was going to, whether he answered the phone or not. He pulled up the message and played it.

"I'm glad you didn't pick up, I was sure you wouldn't," she said. He turned the speaker on and lowered the phone. "I want to say this and I don't want you interrupting me or trying to stop me. I don't want to fight anymore. And as long as I'm in your life, we'll be fighting, 'cause you know I'm never gonna get clean. I'm a prisoner for life, and you're too good to be locked up with me." He could hear her breath stuttering from crying. He didn't like where the message was going.

"I'm a fuck-up. I'll always be a fuck-up. I can't imagine being anything else." She paused, and Jake could hear her breathing heavily. Glass smashed in the background. "I'm trying to say I wanna die. I need to be done. And this …" she struggled to get the next sentence out.

"This … this isn't a scheme to get sympathy from you or a way to make you feel like a jerk. You've been perfect. Always. And I've been a disease. I'm going to die tonight, and this is my good-bye. I'm sorry I have to deliver it through a voicemail message, but I couldn't give you the chance to talk me out of it. It wouldn't have worked anyway, and you would have had to go through the rest of your life knowing that your last chance to save me failed. This way is better. Please don't hate me. Please don't remember me like this. And don't try to find me. I love you Jake, I'm sorry I stole your life. I'm sorry I was a—" The message ended. The time limit had run out.

"No, no, no, no," he said, shaking his head. He felt like the ground had just disappeared from underneath him. He called her back, his fingers struggling to navigate through the phone's menu. There was no response, only her voicemail greeting.

"Hey there! You've reached Faith, or actually, you've tried to reach Faith but didn't. Sorry! I'm off in Wonderland having a tea party with the Mad Hatter right now. Or I'm in the shower or something boring like that. Either way, leave me something good!"

Beep.

"Faith, if this is some kind of game, it's not funny. Please call me back. If you're serious, then you need to know that this is not the answer. Please ... please call me back before you do anything you'll regret. I love you. If this is because of what I said earlier, I was just angry. You know how we get. Please Faith, you have to talk to me. Please. I couldn't ... just ... I love you. For Christ's sake don't do this."

He hung up the phone, his mind racing. Her words echoed in his head.

Don't try to find me.

And so he set off to find her.

Jake knew she had left the message from her apartment. This was because she lived near the warehouse of a large grocery store chain, and trucks passed her home at all hours. He heard at least four during her message. That would be his starting place, though he was sure he wouldn't find her there. Or possibly worse, he would.

Fear paralyzed him as he drove. It was a miracle he was able to keep the Pontiac on the road. When he arrived at her apartment, he couldn't even remember the drive over. His head had been too busy replaying her message.

I'm going to die tonight.

Does that mean she's doing something beforehand? He hoped she was. It would give him time to catch up to her, to talk some damn sense into her. He didn't know whether or not he thought her message was legit, but he certainly felt that it was. His thoughts were racing from *how* she would do it to *where* she would do it.

"Please be just fucking around," he cried out as streams ran down his face. He had kept it together up until this point, too focused on getting to her to let emotion set in. He lost it, however, at the thought of her dying alone in an alley somewhere. He tried to convince himself that she was bluffing, despite her insistence that she wasn't. She had strong convictions against ending one's own life, but whether that made her call more or less convincing, he had no idea. They both knew depression first-hand – Jake had inherited it from his mother, Faith developed it after years of abuse – and they often talked about it. It was perhaps the biggest thing they had in common, a shared plight. And two depressed lovers who had known each other for decades were bound to touch on the topic of suicide.

"It's just selfish," she said on one occasion. They were sitting Indian style on her bed. He was sipping a beer while she stroked a stuffed polar bear.

"Oh, is that right?" he replied. "I beg to differ. I think that it's someone's natural right to do it. We should each have the final say in whether we choose to live or not."

"Yeah, if you're a hobo with no family and no responsibilities," she fired back as if she'd been waiting to play that card. "How about a married father of two? What if his family relied on him financially and emotionally? His decision would change the course of their lives. Shit, it could even lead to more suicides."

"Well the mother could always get a job and they could all get counseling," he said in a joking tone.

"Sarcastic bastard," she said, throwing the stuffed bear at him. He raised his arm to block it and a tiny amount of beer splashed him in the face.

"I'm kidding, I get what you're saying." He wiped the liquid off his cheek. "But at the same time, should someone who hates life be obligated to go on living it?"

"They wouldn't be obligated, they could take the easy way out and forsake their responsibilities if they wanted to. But they would die knowing they chose the coward's route and are letting their dependents down. I mean, if a father who was supporting a family packed up his shit and left his wife and kids starving, you would call him an asshole, regardless of his reason," she said, pausing to allow a reply.

"I'm not so sure," he said. She gazed at him with a jokingly evil eye and he gave up. "Fine, I would call him an asshole."

She was satisfied with the admission. "And therefore, regardless of his reasons for offing himself, he would be an asshole for leaving his family high and dry."

"Alright, alright, suicide is selfish. Happy?" he teased, then downed the last of his beer and set it on the night stand. "Of course, suicide can be a very positive thing."

"Oh, I can't wait to hear this," she said sarcastically. "Please enlighten me."

"One word: Hitler," he said with mock pride, as if he had just won some great debate.

She giggled. "Okay, enough of this downer conversation. Take off your clothes and turn off the light."

They had many conversations along those lines. They loved discussing macabre topics. It was strange that dark subjects actually lightened their moods. Some of their most memorable discussions were about death, poverty, depression and anything else that most would consider gloomy. The ironic thing was that these talks never ended in arguments, as many philosophical debates tend to do. Yet a simple talk about what to have for dinner could explode into an epic battle. The fact that they were both touchy and afraid of normal life yet found solace is reflecting upon higher issues had always concerned him.

He climbed out of the Pontiac's window and jetted up the stairs to her apartment on the third floor. The small blood stains were still on the door, just as the dried blood was still on his knuckles. She had recently needed to change the locks – the neighborhood was an unforgiving one – and he didn't have a key yet. If he did, he could have just waltzed in there earlier and he wouldn't be in this mess. He was prepared to kick the door in if needed, but found it to be unlocked.

"Faith!" he yelled into the apartment, not expecting a response. He scanned every room, praying to find them empty. They were. Her bedroom was in complete disarray. It looked as if just that room was raided by police. Clothes and dresser drawers were scattered everywhere, along with photos and papers. Either Faith or someone else was trying real hard to find something in there. He would have been concerned if he hadn't been so glad to not find a body. The empty apartment was a bittersweet discovery.

He searched frantically for her cell phone. He didn't expect to find it, but the contacts stored in it were just about his only hope. He suspected that even if she was seriously considering killing herself, she would want one last fix. Then again, that may have just been the cynic in him. The phone wasn't there, but if he knew Faith, she would never risk losing it and being left without the numbers to her dealers. She had to have them written somewhere. This was the only time he had ever hoped she was heading to one of those lowlife pieces of shit.

He ripped open the drawers in her desk and shuffled through all sorts of junk. Almost too conveniently, he pulled out a daily planner. None of the calendar days had any entries, but sure enough, the contacts section had dozens of names and numbers. If she had gone looking for heroin, she was heading to one of two people.

Paul or Corey, he thought. *Hopefully Corey*.

Corey was a mutual friend of theirs that they had known for years. The truth was, Jake hadn't considered him a friend in a long time. Faith and Corey had gotten into drugs together, and Jake secretly put some of the blame for Faith's condition on him. He was a good person who was just messed up in things he shouldn't have been, and unfortunately he had an influence on her.

If life had taken a slightly different turn, Faith and Corey could have easily ended up together. Jake thought about this often, since it was so obvious, and he was sure the two of them thought about it too. He wondered about where he would be if life had veered onto that path. He wouldn't be so caught up in Faith's downward spiral. He would probably be a family man by now with a career in law that wasn't forced to be put aside for years while he struggled to get his shit in order. It was a nice thought, but he was positive that if the two of them had ended up together, at least one would have been dead by now. Both were daily users and were absolutely horrible to be around when they lacked a supply of dope. They would do anything to get it, and were interested in nothing else when on the hunt for it. What had always scared him the most was that they tended to overcompensate when a long, hard search came to an end. Without a sober companion, they would have never survived as a couple, Jake was positive.

He found Corey's number and dialed it, desperate for her

to be with him, or at least for info on her whereabouts. He did *not* want to be forced to call Paul.

"Hey Jake, what's up," Corey said through the receiver. His speech was slow. He must have been high, he sounded like Jake's call had surprised him as he was nodding off.

"Not much man. Hey, have you heard from Faith today?" he asked hopefully, picking up a smashed photo frame from the floor. In it, he was smiling with Faith beside him. They were at a bar, looking like they were having a grand ol' time.

"Nah, man, not today."

Even if she did call you, you were probably asleep drooling on yourself. He placed the frame on the desk next to him.

"This is serious Corey, I need to know if she's with you. I'm not fucking around."

"Dude, I swear. What's going on? You guys get into a brawl or something?"

"No. Well, yeah but that's not why I need to find her." Jake always got the feeling that Corey loved the idea of them fighting. No doubt wished he was in Jake's shoes. *Then the two of you could be a happy little junkie couple living in a fantasy world and sticking each other with needles all day.* It was a harsh thought to have, but Jake couldn't help but feel contempt for the both of them for making him deal with stupid shit every goddamn day.

"Well, why do you need to find her?" Corey asked, obviously interested in whatever gossip their lives had to offer.

"I'll tell you when I figure it all out, but right now I need to know where she is. Do you have any clue? Anywhere other than—"

"Paul's house bro," Corey interrupted, seemingly aware that it was the last thing Jake wanted to hear. "Sorry man, but I'd say there's like an eighty percent chance she's there, has been there, or will be there."

"Fuck. OK, you can go back to nodding off now," Jake said viciously.

"Man, why you gotta—" Jake hung up before he could finish.

He knew what he had to do and he hated it. In fact, he hated Faith at this moment for putting him in this position. He had to go to Paul's in person, a phone call wouldn't do. Jake wouldn't be able to take his word that she wasn't there.

His throat was terribly dry, since the last thing he had put in his mouth was a chocolate chip cookie forty-five minutes ago. He stopped at the fridge on his way out, hoping there would be a can of soda he could take with him. He wasn't surprised at all to find a completely empty fridge, except for a couple bottles of beer. He opened one, took a swig and left the rest on the counter.

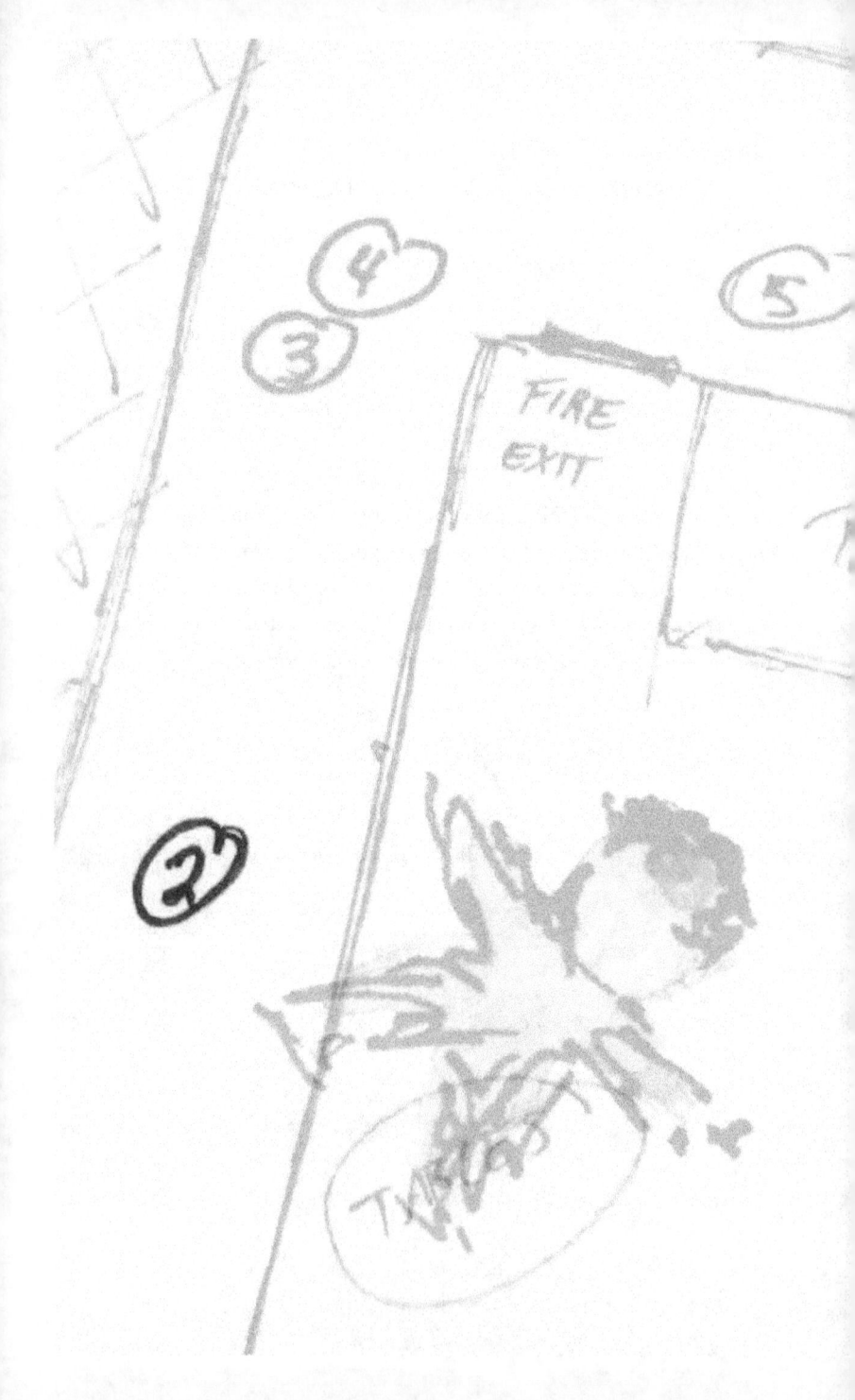

Gabe's Quest

The monsters were coming to take him away from his mother, hiding under the bed was his only defense. He could hear her pleading with the beasts in the kitchen.

"You can't take my baby," she said, more an act of begging than defiance. Her voice was filled with dread but they showed no glimmer of sympathy. Their response was only a series of grunts and growls. His mother couldn't protect him, he knew. The monsters would soon be making their way to his bedroom to snatch him up and take him to a terrible place. The room grew darker. Colors on the wall that were once bright and pastel-colored now turned a dull shade of rust. The saturation of the world around him was drained away, leaving a dreary, hopeless environment in its place. Only a minute ago it was daytime, and sun was oozing into the room through the window. Now it was midnight.

Gabe could hear the footsteps coming slowly his way while his mother shrieked behind them. He could hear her being subdued and his imagination filled in the unknown, placing the worst pictures into his head. They neared the door to his room, each step shaking the house. Picture frames fell off walls, shattering on the floor. He held his breath.

One of the foul creatures turned the corner into his bedroom and its nostrils flared as it took a long breath in through its nose. It was sniffing Gabe out. It stood taller than any man and was covered with hair from head to toe. The hair was black with white patches on its chest and around its wrists. Its hands reminded Gabe of a mole's, large and adorned with gigantic claws made for digging. Or ripping flesh. Eyes devoid of sentimentality scanned the room for its bounty.

There was no chance Gabe could remain hidden. His scent would lead them right to him. He put his hands over his head, too frightened to look upon the grotesque animal any longer. There was a split second of complete silence before the bed above him was thrown aside with the ease of a grizzly bear tossing a pillow. A large, clawed hand grabbed him, threw him into the air and caught him by the leg. It carried him, dangling by his ankle out of his room and toward the front door of the house. This was the end, he knew it.

"My baby!" cried Gabe's mother, on her knees in hysterics. There were four of the vile things including the one carrying him. They all growled, hissed and snarled in unison, then circled her like lions around a wounded gazelle. "I love you Gabe, don't ever forget that. I'll find you. I'll get you back," she yelled.

Gabe tried to shout back, to tell her he loved her too, but nothing came out. He had the feeling not of losing his voice, but of never having had one to begin with. He was dragged out the door and the last he saw of his mother before it was closed was her hand reaching for freedom through a mass of terrible attackers. He heard her screaming in pain and desperation. Then she was devoured.

Gabe woke up.

He was in a daze, and it took him twenty seconds or so to recall what he had been doing before he fell asleep.

Gabe was eleven years old, and a narcoleptic. Consciousness could leave him at any time, though it mostly only happened when his moods shifted dramatically. When he woke from these episodes, there was usually a period of disorientation lasting anywhere from a few seconds to a few minutes.

This had just happened to him, the result of reading a letter. It had excited him so extremely that his entire body ceased to keep him aware, and he fell backwards to the floor. That paper was still in his hand, crinkled now from his involuntary squeezing during the dream.

He had only made it through a third of the message before his high emotions dropped him. He continued reading it now, starting from the beginning to refresh his memory.

Dear Mr. and Mrs. Morrison,

I have tried writing you letters over the years, but I was always paralyzed by fear. I didn't think I deserved the right to appeal to you, but I am now strong enough to make a positive step. I know I have failed as a mother to Gabriel, and nothing will ever set things right. I can only hope that he is in good hands with a loving family who can give him everything I couldn't and still can't. I had him when I was young, and I had no support or help around me when he came into this world. I wasn't ready for the responsibility and because of this, Gabriel was taken from me. It hurts to say it was for the best. My only wish is to be involved with his life in some way, to get the chance to know him. An hour every week or two would mean the world to me. Anything. Please ask him if he would like that. If he's not comfortable with it, then so be it, maybe I'll try again in a few years. Please write back, regardless of your decision. I don't think I'll sleep until I know. Thank you for all you're doing for my boy.

Faith Austen

He knew it. He knew his mother cared about him, even after all these years. And here was the evidence, tucked into Allie's desk.

Jack and Allie Morrison had adopted Gabe when he was six years old. They were great parents who couldn't have their own baby for reasons he didn't understand. And so they brought him in and made him their son. Five years later they were as happy as a family could hope to be. Allie was a college professor and writer. She was amazingly intelligent and Gabe was sure she knew every fact in the universe. She was a plain but subtly beautiful brunette who was the definition of class. Jack was a mechanic who had a scruffy exterior but was made of marshmallow inside. What he lacked in scholastics he made up for in ingenuity. He could fix anything with anything. Gabe tested his skills constantly with abused toys.

He didn't remember his life before being adopted, but the Morrisons told him that he had been with a few foster families before they came along. They were always uneasy when the subject of his past came up. They tended to remain ambiguous and he never learned much about his real parents or why he was no longer with them. It wasn't for a lack of asking, but his questions were always pushed aside and treated as unimportant matters of detail. His mother's first name was just about all he had known until today. Now he knew her last name as well.

He discovered the letter in Allie's office, folded and hidden away in a desk drawer. Gabe hated the thought that the Morrisons weren't going to share the correspondence with him. He ached to know his real mother. He felt it was his right, and resented being treated like a piece of glass that needed to be handled carefully so as not to be broken. Jack and Allie were always too protective, and his gap of knowledge about his early life ate at him. They kept secrets from him.

This was his chance to connect the dots. The return address on the envelope was that of an adoption agency, but his mother *had* included her contact info at the bottom of the letter – including her home address. Jack and Allie were out and the babysitter was so wrapped up in a phone conversation that he could walk a giraffe through the room without her noticing. He could easily grab a few necessities, make a quick exit and embark on his journey to collect missing puzzle pieces. He would show the Morrisons that he was adult enough to be able to handle his true past. The thought of an adventure exhilarated him almost as much as the prospect of meeting his mother.

He moved quietly throughout the house collecting any items he thought he would need for his quest. Into a backpack he threw a few granola bars, a can of soda, a flashlight, a pen and pad, and a folded page containing a speech that Allie had written for a college commencement address – which he was positive was lucky and protected him. He picked the home phone up and listened to make sure the babysitter was using her cell phone to blab on about her relationship woes. After confirming the land line was clear, he ruffled through a phone book and found the number of a cab company. He dialed the number feebly.

After three minutes of convincing the operator that there would be an adult with him for the ride, a taxi was sent to Gabe's home. He easily crept out the front door and waited outside, and a short while later the cab arrived. The driver wasn't happy when he saw only an unsupervised eleven-year-old waiting to hop in.

He gawked at Gabe through the open passenger-side window. "Where's your parents, kid?" he asked in a tone that really said, "You better not get in this cab all by yourself." He took three rapid puffs from a large cigar. He was husky with a bald head and a red polo shirt that was too tight and showed signs of sweat. He wore huge sunglasses, and Gabe thought they made him look like a bug.

"There was an emergency and my mother had to go, but I still need the ride," he lied.

"Oh, no, no, no, no, no, no," the driver shook his head and waved his finger. "I don't friggin' think so. Sorry buddy, but my ass is grass if I let you get in this car." He faced forward and put his hand on the shifter.

Gabe spoke quickly, "My mother knew you'd say that. She said to tell you that I'll tip you twice the amount of the fare if you bring me." He was delighted by how easily the lie came out. All his life he had played the part of the shy kid, finding it difficult to talk to people he wasn't comfortable with. Gabe had practiced the line out loud before the driver pulled up, afraid that his timidity wouldn't let him pull it off. He was proud of his little con, and was now confident it would go off without a hitch.

"You call that a bribe?" The driver chuckled and shook his head.

Gabe's confidence waned. "She also told me that might not work and to up it to five times if I needed to." Gabe hoped not only that the driver would accept, but that his three hundred dollars would cover it. Every day for school, Gabe was given four dollars for lunch and only used two. He had been saving for a while now, which netted him two hundred. The other hundred he took from the babysitter's purse on his way out. He had never stolen anything, but this time it was a necessary evil.

"Where you going?" the driver asked, his decision hinging on whether the trip would bring in a decent amount. "I'm not taking twenty dollars to drive a kid ten blocks."

"It's 322 Baker Avenue, in Canterville." Gabe was looking down at the sidewalk, fidgeting. The journey couldn't end here, before it even started. It just couldn't. He didn't know where Eastbridge was, but he hoped it was far enough to be worthwhile for the driver.

"Canterville!?" The driver's eyes lit up, and his cigar almost dropped from his mouth. "Hop in kid." Gabe ecstatically climbed into the back seat while the driver plugged the address into his GPS navigation. "Looks like some apartments. Why you headed halfway across the state to an apartment complex?" He shifted the car into drive and reset the meter.

"I'm going to visit family," Gabe said, thinking afterwards that it was a lame excuse and he should have been more prepared for the question. Then he added, "And I might fall asleep on the way over. I'm a little tired. If I do, just wake me up when we get there." Gabe thought it best to cover himself in case his narcolepsy struck. The driver was already uneasy about his passenger, and a medical condition wouldn't have helped his discomfort. Not that a sleeping eleven-year-old on a long trip would have surprised many adults. Either way, immediately following his forewarning, the excitement of the quest got the better of him. He felt a dull pain in his joints and his vision began to blur. Fighting it would be useless and there was no harm in giving in. He dropped his head and fell asleep.

He was surrounded by men in masks. No two were the same. They towered over him, forming a dome he couldn't break out from. One wore a masquerade mask that only covered the top half of his face. Black swirls curled over the dark red porcelain pointing towards two dark holes that housed hidden eyes. Another face was covered with an African tribal mask made of wood. Perfectly round holes riddled the surface, the work of some exotic insect. The third and final enemy wore a rubber clown mask sporting a demonic smile outlined in red and white paint. They jabbed at him with a rapier, a sharpened stick and a machete, respectively.

The stabs didn't draw blood. Instead, a piece of his soul leaked out and rose like green smoke until it disappeared above him. He tried to grab the pieces to put them back in, but they just swirled around his fingers. Meanwhile more holes were being opened by jabs, and more soul was spilling out. The assaulters laughed maniacally while they did this.

They were in a house, in a living room. The world around them was black and white only, not a trace of color visible aside from the terrifying masks and Gabe's soul. He didn't know why he was in the house, he didn't belong there. Nor did he know why he was being prodded maliciously.

It was strange – even though he couldn't remember this happening before, he knew it had, and often. He was drowned in the ever present fear of the masked assailants catching him alone. And here they were again, his eternal tormentors. He dropped to the ground, completely emptied of his soul. He looked up at the smoky cloud hovering above. At once, all three breathed in deeply, and the green smoke was sucked into their mouths. They stopped their attack. His soul was all they wanted, and they had taken all he had to give. He wished he could remain drained so they would never come back, but soon his soul would replenish, and they would return for another helping.

He lay there, soulless, hopeless and hapless. His mother was gone, he had no protection. No friends to pull him from clutches of the masked men. A strange, faceless woman appeared often, but she was no help. When she showed up, the masked men turned to angels. Their disguises would melt away as white feathered wings sprouted from their backs. Color would return to the environment for a time, but these transformations were temporary. As soon as she left again, their ruthlessness returned. He didn't dare tell the woman of their deeds. That would only make it worse. She wouldn't believe any slander against her angels, and in her absence they would resume their masked identities, and the punishment would be tenfold. Instead, he stood his ground and endured their harassment, hoping that he would soon be swept away and rescued.

They were gone now and he lay crying in the dark. A wild wolf appeared and strode majestically to his side. It stood six feet tall on all fours and donned a magnificent coat of red and orange. It didn't speak, much to Gabe's dismay, but did lay against him. This brought Gabe comfort. He liked the wolf, and even though there were never any words spoken between them, he knew the great beast felt his pain. If only it would defend him, the masked men would be kept at bay. It was a gentle animal though, never turning to violence despite its stature and deadly potential.

As he huddled close to the beast, he could feel the warmth inside of him that meant his soul was returning. It wouldn't be long now before he would once again be jabbed viciously. For now, though, he enjoyed the company he had with the enormous creature acting as his pillow.

"Hey kid," the driver said softly, "wake up, we're a few minutes away."

Gabe rubbed his eyes and focused hard on remembering where he was and what he was doing. He looked to his side, expecting to find the great wolf. He was disappointed. The dreams he fell into during his episodes were far more vivid than normal ones. There was a feeling of deja vu that hung over them, regardless of how far-fetched they were, and he almost always woke disoriented. He regained his composure.

"Could you drop me off about a mile away, please?" Gabe didn't know what his destination would bring and didn't want an attention-grabbing yellow cab to give away his arrival.

"Whatever you say pal." Gabe had expected the driver to push back at that. He was relieved that he didn't need to make a case for the request. "This is as good a spot as any, I need a drink," the driver said, pulling up to a convenience store.

They both got out of the car. The low sun struck Gabe sharply, his eyes not yet recovered from sleep. "Thank you sir," he said, closing the car door.

"You sure you don't wanna just let me take you the rest of the way?" the driver said, coming around the front of the cab. Now that he was out of the car, Gabe noticed he waddled a bit, reminding him of a penguin. Normally, he would have giggled. "My conscience doesn't like letting a kid go walking alone down a busy street."

"I'll be fine, it's only a mile. I'll be there in fifteen minutes." Gabe liked the driver, he felt comfortable talking to him. It was new to him. He generally kept silent around new people.

He pulled out his two hundred dollar savings. He didn't know if it would cover the large tip he'd promised the man, but he needed to keep the babysitter's hundred just in case there were further expenses. He handed it to the driver, hoping for the best. The man gave Gabe an interrogative stare.

"Be honest, little one. Is that your money or your parents'?"

Gabe didn't know what the best response would be, so he stuck with the truth. "Mine. I've been saving up in case I needed something a really lot, and I needed this ride more than anything." He hoped that was all he would have to say about that. He didn't want to share the details of his mission.

The man sighed and scratched his head. "Then forget about the deal, just pay me the straight fare, kid. I wouldn't be able to sleep at night knowin' I took a young man's savings. A hundred and twenty bucks'll do it." Gabe happily handed it over, overjoyed that he wasn't called out on the fact that he didn't have five times that amount, whatever it might be. "You take care now," the man said with a smile, then headed toward the door of the store.

As soon as Gabe turned around, he was startled by a woman who looked like she had been to Hell and back. She addressed him as if they knew each other. They surely didn't.

"Hey there hun, what's got a young'n like you taking a cab ride long enough to rack up a fare that high?" Gabe was not only taken aback by her appearance – which was downright atrocious – but was also weary of the fact that she was interrogating him about things she had no business knowing. She looked disturbed and dirty. Her hair had visible tangles and her ebony face showed paranoia. A dirty purple tank top covered her upper body, and Gabe was sure there were blood stains peppered around the front.

"I'm going to visit family," he responded. The answer had been enough for the cab driver, and had the extra bonus of being true. He found it difficult to look her in the eyes, so he kept his gaze to the ground.

"Uh-huh, and where might this family be?" she said. Gabe felt uneasy about her nosiness and wanted desperately to get out of the conversation, to be on his way. The woman didn't look like she had a tight grip on reality. Her eyes wandered as she spoke and her voice sounded distant. There was a trace of struggle in her face and her jaw clenched between sentences. Gabe thought maybe she had Tourette Syndrome and was fighting back the urge to swear at him. It was either that or she was possessed. He preferred to assume it was Tourette's.

"Just down the street, in an apartment complex," he answered. "I don't know the name of it, but I know it's there."

"Must be The Swan Orchard Apartments," the woman said, her gaze fixed on the store behind Gabe. Then she pointed in the opposite direction, still staring. "Straight down this road on your right. You sure you don't want the cab to just bring you the rest of the way?"

Gabe decided to end this back-and-forth. "I'm sure. I better get going." He walked briskly away from her.

"Alright then, watch yourself young'n," the woman said.

Damn crazies, he thought, then began his trek towards his mother and The Swan Orchard Apartments.

A short while later, Gabe arrived at the apartments, which was exactly where the crazy black lady had told him it would be. The sign, which was very unoriginal, showed two swans swimming in a pond by an orchard. Gabe was sure he could have made a better sign with a few crayons any day.

He pulled out the letter with his mother's address. The apartment number was forty-two. The complex didn't have any intuitive organization that Gabe could tell. After searching aimlessly for a few minutes, he finally found apartment thirty-five by luck, and headed in the direction of higher numbers. He reached the door that read "42," which was terribly stained with all sorts of colors. It blended with the rest of the building, which was densely covered in blemishes. There were random pieces of garbage everywhere. He couldn't imagine why his mother was living in a dump like this. Surely she could do better. He thought perhaps it was a temporary place for her to live. That made sense.

He raised his fist, but froze up in fear before he could knock on the door. He was suddenly filled with doubt. What if she didn't like him? Or if she had other kids?

He walked away from the door and paced in the hallway. He reached into his bag and pulled out the folded piece of paper he had brought along; his good luck charm. It was the draft of a commencement speech that Allie had written and delivered a year earlier. He remembered being in the audience with Jack, watching her address the crowd.

"Anyone can exist," she said, looking at the audience and never down at her paper. "Anyone can function and go on being, that's easy. But that's not living. If one simply functions, their future will just happen without their will having an effect upon it. To be motivated and to be productive is to have control over your future. Life is a game of odds, and the one who merely exists is the gambling addict at the slots parlor. There is no fate more empty than that. The go-getter is the house, taking advantage of those odds. The house always comes out ahead. Never relax and let life happen to you. Never."

He had loved her speech so much that he had gone and plucked the draft from her notebook. He kept it with him and read it regularly. Allie's voice reading it in his head always managed to inspire him.

The advice did the trick, and he was ready to be the house, to knock on the door. He marched back toward it, but it opened suddenly when he was still three apartments away. A tall, majestic blonde emerged from the door and closed it behind her.

He knew instantly that this woman was the reason for his adventure. He had a gut feeling that this was indeed his mother, and the sight of her had him in awe. She looked like a queen, with a stature that demanded respect. Her blonde hair would have been perfect for a crown to sit upon. Gabe was surprised to see a large scar across her forehead. No doubt there was a story of some heroic deed behind it. He was filled with wishes of catching up with her, of going to the park and the zoo, of having fun with her.

She seemed to be in a rush, but noticed Gabe out of the corner of her eye and turned to glance at him. When their eyes met, he froze once again and could do nothing but stand there and stare.

A second later, after giving him a confused look, she turned and walked away toward the exit of the building. Gabe followed her, dodging trash bags on his way. The place was downright filthy, not fit for a pig, let alone a queen. He kept his distance. The one thing he hadn't thought through was what he would say to her. He realized his lack of preparation now. As he reached the parking lot, he heard a commotion. His eyes swept the area and he realized that someone was yelling at his mother.

"Mind your own business," she yelled back at the person, who Gabe couldn't see at the moment. He hadn't heard the start of the exchange, but there was no way his mother could have been in the wrong. She was too perfect for that. He crept out a bit and saw her standing by the open door to a green truck, ready to get in but distracted by a large man a few parking spots away. The man looked trashy to Gabe. He wore a gray t-shirt, gray sweatpants and sandals. After seeing the crazy lady at the convenience store and this piece of work, he didn't have high opinions of the people in the area.

"When I can hear your bullshit from four apartments away, it *is* my business," the man replied from behind the large paper shopping bag he was carrying. He clearly didn't understand who he was talking to. Gabe wanted to hurt him for having the audacity to cuss at his mother. She walked toward the man in a confrontational manner.

"If you didn't like my 'bullshit,' then you should've talked to the property managers or moved." Gabe seized the opportunity and climbed into the bed of her pickup truck. He didn't know what his next step should be or how he would approach her, so the best option was to stick with her until he figured it out. He hoped something would come to mind.

"Oh, you can bet your ass I'm going to talk to the managers, and I'll be the hero of the complex for doing it. Everyone here is sick and tired of hearing you and your boyfriend fight every other damn day." Gabe could hear the man's voice waver a bit at her approach. The thought of his mother intimidating a man that large made him proud. He laid down and tucked himself close to the wall of the bed. It would have made for an awkward meeting if she found him there. Their reunion needed to be much more graceful than that. He hoped he was concealed enough.

"Well you won't have to hear it anymore," she retorted. "I'm never coming back to this fucking cesspool." Gabe was satisfied to hear her verify his theory. He knew this place was short-term for her.

"And thank God for that. No one'll miss you, trust me."

"Feeling's mutual, prick." He heard her footsteps approaching the truck. He held his breath and clung to the side. She hopped in the driver's seat and started it up. Gabe let out his breath.

"Fucking dopehead bitch," Gabe heard the man say, but was sure she didn't catch it.

The truck pulled out of the parking lot in a fury, giving him a good indication of his mother's mood. It would be better if he waited for her state of mind to brighten before introducing himself.

He began thinking of his current situation, which made his heart beat faster. He was in the bed of a stranger's truck. On top of that, the truck was moving and he had no notion of its destination. For the first time in his short journey, he became worried of its outcome. The worrying elevated his heart rate, which in turn worried him, and thus elevated it more. The cycle made him feel dizzy. He wasn't afraid for his health – this sort of thing, while not very common, had happened to him many times. He was afraid of what it would mean to his quest, since he'd be unconscious soon if he didn't calm down. He dreaded the idea of his mother leaving the truck before he woke up. Or even worse, she could discover him sleeping and he wouldn't be able to explain himself. These thoughts pushed his anxiety over the edge. His breathing increased to a rapid rate, then he was out.

FIRE
EXIT

Adrien's Kill, Amy's Trouble

He did it again, Amy thought, standing over a corpse in a business suit. Half dressed in the suit, actually. He had been in the middle of taking his pants off for Amy when Adrien appeared and stabbed him in the throat with a Swiss army knife.

And he never has to deal with the aftermath. It's always up to me. Prick. And if Ron finds out another one of his clients is dead, he's gonna bury me. I need to get the hell outta here, and fast. I can't ever come back.

Amy was shaking at the thought of Ron getting his hands on her after this. Ron was her pimp, and the unlucky dead guy with his pants around his ankles was a paying customer. This turn of events would most likely get Amy killed, she knew that. The best she could possibly hope for was a broken jaw, but she wasn't an optimistic person by nature and Ron wasn't a lenient one. He wouldn't care that it was Adrien that had killed the client. It was all the same to him. Amy would take the brunt of the punishment.

She was with Adrien's newest victim in an apartment that Ron rented for the sole purposes of helping men get their rocks off. He wasn't helping them for nothing, of course. Their pleasure earned him a very comfortable living and did little more for his girls than to put food in their mouths.

The apartment was a studio with just enough room for a mattress and a refrigerator. And that's all it had in it, besides cockroaches, ripped wallpaper and more stains than a person could count. Now it also had a dead man and a puddle of blood on the floor. The customer – whose name she didn't want to know – was hanging off the mattress, half on the floor. His neck was opened and dripping.

And he was actually kind of nice, she thought. *Damn shame.*

Adrien left dead bodies around Amy regularly and forced her to clean up the messes so that their secret would remain a secret. He was a demon that lived in Amy's head. At least that's what she thought he was. No, what she *knew* he was. Of course the doctors all thought she was just schizophrenic. *Knew* she was schizophrenic. She wished the same upon them, a demon in their heads. Then they could know what it was like to lose control and have your body used as a tool. It made for a terrible, terrible life.

"And where are you now Adrien, huh? Can't face your own dirty work?" she said. She wasn't confrontational, but she had no problem expressing her discontent with him. He was with her constantly, his presence a burden even when he was silent. He spoke now, taking hold of Amy's mouth and throat.

"I can face it just fine, and it just so happens that the work was pure, not dirty. How many times do I have to tell you that, you pitiful bitch?"

Amy knew why people thought she was crazy. To them, she was always talking to herself in different voices. She wished Adrien would just keep quiet, but he always felt the need to use her own mouth to speak to her. Even after all the experience she had with it, she still felt unnerved.

"But he was a nice one, he didn't wanna hurt me none," she responded, knowing that her criticism was like pebbles being thrown at a shark. "But you just gotta come in and screw everything up real nice for me whenever you get an itch."

"No, of course he didn't want to hurt you. He only wanted to fuck you and give Ron a few measly dollars that you would never see. He was a sweetie, I'm sure. You're a dumb cunt, you know that? He deserved to die just like every other john and murderer and rapist and fraud and bully and pedophile and junkie in this shit hole world." Amy's entire life was now based on this philosophy. Adrien killed whoever he felt was unworthy to walk the earth and cussed at her when she questioned it. She lived with a constant negativity that would have driven the Dalai Lama to madness.

She hated Adrien, but she couldn't help sometimes feeling that he was right. He never killed innocents, though his idea of justice rarely fit the crime. She was generally disgusted by his acts, but there were occasional feelings of satisfaction in her when he put down a real piece of shit. Most times, though, it didn't sit right with her at all. Like now. And it was always a real fucking hassle for her to try to keep his slaughters hidden, especially when the urge struck him in public. There had been too many close calls to count.

Just the day before, he had stalked and killed a man who had been accused of killing a young boy. Amy's feelings toward that one were conflicted. He might not have been guilty – but if he was, she would find it hard to be affected by his death.

"Why did you have to go and do it there?" she asked Adrien,

sprinting from the scene. She was terrified that someone might have seen them. "You sure got some backwards-ass thinking."

"I did it there because I could, now shut your whore mouth and get us out of here," he spit back at her.

"Sometimes I swear you just tryin' to get us both locked up. That man might not have even done nothing."

Minutes earlier Adrien had used her to ask the man for the time.

"Quarter past two," the man said cautiously, clearly seeing something disturbing in her eyes. He looked upper-class, with a suit jacket covering his sweater vest. Amy and Adrien had spotted the story of his arrest and pending trial in the paper a few days earlier. Adrien hadn't stopped buzzing until he found out the man's address and tracked him down. He confronted the man at last, transforming Amy's sweet voice into a devilish, accusatory growl.

"Thanks, and could you also tell me what gives you the right to take the life of a nine-year-old boy?" The man was shocked. That was perhaps the last thing he ever expected to hear from her.

"I'm appalled you would say such a … who are you?"

"A man with a taser and a knife who's gonna stun you and slit your throat." She could feel Adrien's excitement and anticipation. "And the world's gonna move on just fine – better in fact, with one less savage carrying on like the world is his oyster."

"A *man*?" he responded, not understanding what was happening. "But you're a woman."

"Typical inept human. Caught up on trivia while issues of great importance are on the table." He reached into Amy's bag and pulled out a taser. The man turned and started to run.

Adrien threw Amy's hands out and grabbed the man by his

collar, then shoved the taser into his back. He fell to the ground, making a gurgling noise on the way down. Adrien opened a butterfly knife and straddled the man. He was laughing maniacally and Amy could feel her throat being abused. It hurt immensely.

"Now you die, and the world will thank me," Adrien said and dragged the knife across the man's neck. He closed Amy's eyes and let his victim's last sounds wash over him. Amy wasn't a killer, could barely stand being put through this. The dying gurgles emanating from the soon-to-be-dead man would have made her cry if she had control of her body. She was thankful Adrien wasn't looking at the man as well. She didn't want to see it.

She tried to talk to Adrien, but couldn't get control of her mouth. Instead, she let her thoughts do the communicating.

Can we leave now, please? Someone's gonna see us. And if I get caught, you're in trouble too.

"Almost," he responded. "You know what I have to do first." She *did* know, and it disturbed her every time.

He dipped her finger in the man's blood which was pooling on the asphalt, and put two dots under each of the man's eyes. It was a ritual that he did after each kill. He called it "making them weep." She had asked him about it before, but his response was telling her to shut the fuck up and know her place.

He had done that same thing with the blood in the apartment, to Ron's client. Then he relinquished control to Amy. Now she had to come up with a plan and hope he didn't get in the way or make more trouble for her. She couldn't go to Ron, so that basically meant leaving town. If that was the case, there was no use covering this up. If anything, the apartment would be traced to

Ron and she wouldn't be on the law's radar. She grabbed the man's wallet and snatched the money out of it without even looking at his driver's license. The last thing she wanted to do was to put a name to this lifeless face. She was tossing the wallet aside when she heard a commotion in the hallway.

"Awww come on Faith, let me in," someone in the hallway said, sounding exhausted. Amy peeked through the peep hole and saw that the ruckus was coming from right outside. There was a young man in a blue baseball jersey in the hall talking through the opposite apartment's door.

"I'm not letting you in, so just fucking leave already!" It was the woman who lived there, yelling at him from inside. Amy had never seen her, but she overheard quite a few bouts. The girl was on drugs, or so Amy could ascertain from the back-and-forths of the two. She felt bad for her. Adrien wanted to kill her.

"Fine you junkie bitch, don't open the door," the man, who looked to Amy to be in his late twenties, yelled. "Just sit in there and stick another shot of fake bliss into your fucking arm!"

Amy needed this like a bullet in the rib. Any other time she would have been glad to see a bit of drama. Free entertainment was just fine with her. Unfortunately, Ron would be expecting to hear from her and would come around if he didn't. She needed this to wrap up quickly.

"I'm not doping, you asshole, I just don't wanna talk to you," the girl said back to him. Then she yelled suddenly, as if possessed with her very own Adrien, "And if you ever call me a junkie bitch again I'll cut your fucking balls off and feed them to you! Now get the fuck out of here before one of my neighbors calls the cops!"

Won't be me calling no cops, that's for damn sure.

Bang!

The man punched the door, startling Amy a bit. The light fixture behind her rattled. He left hurriedly after his display of aggression. She was grateful for that.

"Wish I could gut that fucking junkie," Adrien said.

"Oh, come on Adrien. There's no need to go hurtin' her just cause she's got herself an addiction. She could be a good person inside." This would get him going.

"Doesn't matter, she's still bringing your society down. I bet she'd steal from her own mother for a fix. Is that the kind of creature you would want around your kids? Assuming Ron would ever let you have any, that fucking prick."

"I guess not," she said, grabbing her backpack and the Swiss army knife. "But that doesn't mean she needs to die." She wiped the blade off on the mattress. "And I never asked you 'bout this before – but speaking of Ron, how come you never tried to kill him? He's as bad as anyone. I know you don't like him none."

"I've never killed Ron," Adrien responded, annoyed, "because he keeps us fed. But don't think I don't want to. He's a means to an end. I know damn well what I'm doing. I know in your dumb fucking head you think I'm not rational, but I am. I'm sure you think all sorts of nasty things about me, don't you whore?"

Something Amy never quite understood about Adrien was this: he didn't seem to be able to read her mind unless she actively spoke to him through it. If she directed her thoughts at him, he heard her, yet she was able to have privacy in her head when she wished. This seemed nonsensical to her, since he could control her as if he were holding a remote. He had a button for her fingers, her arms, her mouth, eyes, nose, legs and just about every other body part. He apparently didn't get any feedback from his puppet though, since she could think whatever she wanted at any time and he hadn't the slightest clue about it. She was thoroughly happy about that, since Adrien wouldn't have liked her thoughts. If he *did* know what she was thinking, every waking minute would have been filled with his two cents on every subject that crossed her mind. She would have eaten a bullet long ago.

"I don't think no negative or nasty things about you Adrien. Why would I, you being such a warm, snuggly person and all?" she said, egging him on. She was genuinely unafraid of him, despite what he was. His survival hinged on hers. She had immunity from him, but that didn't stop him from threatening her with every chance he got.

"Don't get wise with me you worthless twit. I'd rip your insides out with your own fucking hands if I didn't need you."

Amy was soon walking along the street a half mile from The Swan Orchard Apartment Complex with her thumb out. Adrien had apparently decided to give her some quiet time. She'd heard enough from him for one day anyway, so she was glad for that. She had no idea where she should hitch a ride to, so her plan was to just go as far as her driver would take her.

Maybe lady luck'll be in my favor and I'll get picked up by a driver going real far. Like Texas or Canada, or some other place I ain't never been to.

Amy was a twenty-one-year-old orphan. Before life with Adrien, she had been spunky. She had fun. She grew up poor, but her spirits never suffered from it. Her parents couldn't afford much more than their apartment in the projects, so she was accustomed to living with only necessities. Many times not even that much. It was a warm family though, and she had been close to her parents and younger brother. When she was sixteen, the three of them were killed by an intoxicated driver. It was eleven o'clock in the morning, yet the driver had a soda bottle filled with whisky in the cup holder. Her brother was only seven years old.

There were no remaining family members to be her guardian, so Amy was put into a foster home. She ran away a day later and never returned. She'd been living on her own for five years, the whole time working for Ron to pay for her tiny apartment. She had seen and done things at seventeen years old that no one should experience. Her life was pain. In the face her tragedies, however, she was always upbeat and cheerful. She had an easy time making friends and all of Ron's other girls who knew her loved her even though internal scuffles were the norm.

Then she was infested with a demon.

Adrien intruded into her head about two years ago. Once he showed up, he was with her almost daily, except for the couple months in the hospital where he didn't say a word. Those were a good two months for Amy. She didn't understand the workings of demons, so she didn't care to theorize on how or why he had invited himself inside of her. She had asked him about it once. He swore and threatened to kill her.

The first time Adrien made himself known was during a second date Amy had with a fitness instructor named Nathan. Nathan had done a bang-up job with their first date, so Amy was particularly girlish on the follow-up. He was also an orphan, and a damn handsome one at that. Amy's job kept her from seeing many men as attractive, but she couldn't believe her good fortune at hooking one so gorgeous. They were enjoying themselves at a drive-in movie. It was a double feature and the first movie had just ended. It was some teen comedy about a group of high school friends who learn the secret of the universe and use it to mess with people. It was truly terrible, but the next one was a horror film that the two of them were eager to see.

There was a twenty-minute intermission between the movies for people to use the bathroom, get snacks, get laid, or anything else they could care to do in twenty minutes. Neither Amy nor Nathan had to use the bathroom. They also had a cooler full of snacks and drinks, and had each been laid twice that day – once with each other, once earlier without. So they spent their twenty-minute intermission talking.

"That was undoubtedly the dumbest movie I've ever sat through," Nathan said, tossing a piece of popcorn in the air and missing it with his mouth. "And on top of that, it was offensive to nerds, and that's coming from someone who would know. It's like they just scoured the internet for *Star Trek* and string theory references and wrote it into the dialogue to turn the geeky characters into space trivia recordings. A one-trick pony if I've ever seen one, and the pony sucked to begin with."

Amy snatched the missed popcorn off his shirt and tossed it into her mouth. "Well I didn't get the whole geek-hating vibe that you did and I sure as hell didn't see any ponies, but it still sucked." They both gave a small chuckle.

"So, you wanna smoke a joint or something?" Nathan asked sheepishly, not sure if she would be into the idea or not.

"Yeah I'm down for that. You need papers or …?" Amy didn't know why she was asking, she didn't have any to offer.

"Nah, I got a few pre-rolled." Nathan pulled out a pack of cigarettes and opened it. There were two cigarettes alongside three joints. There was something else in the pack taking up the rest of the space, but it was too short to see it behind the sides of the box. The mystery item caught Amy's attention. Then, as if pushed by her stare, the pack fell onto his lap. He snatched it up with a quick reaction.

The drop was a foot at most, but that short distance let her see what was in the cigarette pack. It was a small liquid prescription bottle. She knew instantly what it was. Even if she'd never seen it in person, all the girls from her high-school had been taught about it in sex ed. The sight of it introduced her to Adrien.

Weeks later, Amy would describe the moment to her doctor. "It was like I had been driving a terribly uncomfortable car going on two days. I'd been tired at the wheel for a long time, but I had nowhere to stop, so I kept on. Then, seconds before I fell asleep and crashed, someone took over the wheel and let me rest. Adrien just popped up out of nowhere and drove for me."

Adrien's first words nearly made Nathan jump through his car window.

"I know that shit ain't for Amy, since that bitch is willingly givin' it up to you," the new voice said. It was harsh and raspy. "So why don't you tell me who's fucking drink you're lacing. You get off on fucking unconscious girls?"

"I ... uh, it's not—" Nathan stuttered. He was too scared to speak and Amy could feel this new person inside of her soaking it up.

"Bullshit it's not, you wretched little mongrel." Before Nathan could defend himself, Adrien grabbed a fork they had used to eat chicken fried rice with during the last movie and shoved it into his left eye. He howled in pain. Amy could do nothing but stand by in her own mind, surprised and dumbfounded with what was going on. She was afraid, both for him and for herself. Seconds ago they were having fun, now there was only terror.

The commotion drew attention immediately from the crowd around the car and people quickly approached them. Adrien hit the automatic door locks to stall them a few seconds. He ripped the fork free and jammed it in Nathan's throat, aiming for his Adam's apple. The poor, dying kid grabbed Amy's face in a panic, his eyes and mouth both wide open. She wanted so badly to help him, but her body was no longer hers to command.

People outside of the car were now banging on the windows. One strike made it through and shattered the glass behind Amy. A large man hit it repeatedly to clear the shards and pulled her out by the shoulders. That was the last she remembered before waking up in a jail cell covered in blood.

Amy continued walking with her thumb held high, fearing that no one would pick her up. She was now about a mile from the apartment without anyone so much as considering letting her ride shotgun. She saw a taxi pull up to a convenience store across the street. This was fortunate for her, since she was starting to concede that if she wanted to get anywhere, she would have to pay for it.

She crossed the street without looking both ways and made her way to the cab. She noticed the driver already had a passenger, but they were both getting out of the car. To her surprise, the passenger was a boy no older than twelve. He was a cute kid with short, spiky blonde hair. He wore a red t-shirt with a small Spider-man patch on the chest and had a backpack on. She caught the end of their conversation as she neared them.

"Then forget about the deal," the driver said. "Just pay me the straight fare, kid. I wouldn't be able to sleep at night knowin' I took a young man's savings. A hundred and twenty bucks'll do it." Amy was awfully interested in the reason this boy would come far enough to accrue a fare like that. The boy counted the amount and handed it over. "You take care now," the driver said, then walked into the store.

Amy, out of simple curiosity approached the boy.

"Hey there hun, what's got a young'n like you taking a cab ride long enough to rack up a fare that high?"

"I'm going to visit family," the kid responded, startled and slightly confused by her interest. His response sounded to Amy like one he'd thought of in case a stranger came asking questions. He'd probably said the exact same thing to the cab driver.

"Uh-huh, and where might this family be?"

"Just down the street, in an apartment complex. I don't know the name of it, but I know it's there."

"Must be The Swan Orchard Apartments," Amy said, noting the coincidence. "Straight down this road on your right. You sure you don't want the cab to just bring you the rest of the way?" She was concerned for the kid. This was far from the worst part of the city – it was no Orange District – but it still wasn't a place for unattended children.

"I'm sure," the boy said, starting to walk away from this conversation. "I better get going." She could tell she had frightened the kid. Even when she tried being nice, she knew people could see in her eyes that there was trouble in her.

"Alright then, watch yourself young'n," she said, then leaned against the outside of the store to wait for the driver. He came out a minute later with a bag of chocolate covered pretzels and a diet cola. He was startled a bit when she approached him. He was a portly man with a funny walk. His shape, waddle, sweat-damped shirt and food-filled hands made quite a caricature.

"Lookin' for a fare?" Amy said.

"Times are tough, darling. I'm always looking for a fare."

Faith's Decision

"Fine you junkie bitch, don't open the door," Jake spit from outside the apartment. "Just sit in there and stick another shot of fake bliss into your fucking arm!"

His venomous words hit Faith hard. She wished he wasn't right, but he knew her too well. It hadn't been five minutes since she locked him out, and she was already pulling back the plunger, filling the syringe and emptying the spoon. It was the last bit she had and she was afraid it wouldn't even hit her. She wanted to prove Jake wrong, to throw down the needle and let him into the apartment. She didn't. *Couldn't.*

"I'm not doping, you asshole, I just don't wanna talk to you," she said back to him with little conviction. She had never been adept at lying, especially when it was an uphill battle. Knowing she wouldn't succeed in deceiving him, she changed her focus to getting rid of him, yelling, "And if you ever call me a junkie bitch again I'll cut your fucking balls off and feed them to you! Now get the fuck out of here before one of my neighbors calls the cops!" She was confident that would get results. Threats came more naturally to her than lies.

Bang!

She saw the door shake as Jake apparently punched it. It wasn't like him to get violent, so she knew this time she'd struck a nerve. They fought plenty, but their duels usually involved animosity on her part while he tried to diffuse the situation. She would have preferred that he fight back, like he was doing now. The emotion was real, it felt honest. His usual calmness felt like damage control and nothing more. She waited for another fist to strike the door, almost hoping for it, but none came. A minute of silence later, she looked through the peep hole in the door and found that Jake was gone. She decided it was for the best, since her neighbors were surely getting an earful.

With the filled syringe still in hand, she leaned against the wall, slumped to the ground and wept. She eyed the liquid in the chamber with simultaneous feelings of hatred and desire. It owned her life, directed her actions and monopolized her thoughts. It wasn't her fault, though. She didn't ask to be an addict, the life was inevitable for her. She'd hated how people always spoke of destiny idealistically, while her experience with it was completely contrary. Her scumbag father and weak mother led her to this. Fuck nature, nurture made her what she was – a worthless addict crying on the floor with a needle in her hand.

And yet her parents were no longer involved in her life, so what excuse did she have left? Was the damage irreversible, leaving her to repeat her mistakes? It seemed that way. Her past blocked the light from her life. Sunshine was muted, time with loved ones was tainted by guilt, fun was nonexistent. Life was poison, except for the precious highs she could scrape together. Heroin exacerbated her problems, but was the only ray of light she had left. Jake didn't understand the quandary. Only someone who had known it firsthand could process how important it was to hold on to the one thing that could provide delight, despite the payment it demanded in return. It was her best friend and archenemy rolled into one omnipotent creature granting jubilation one minute, and denying it the next. She had told this to Jake once, and he accused her of romanticizing a plague.

Sitting there on the floor with tears in her eyes, she drove the needle into a vein in her foot. When the chamber was drained, she sat back in silence and stared at the ceiling. Her muscles loosened and her limbs became unresponsive. All was set right in that moment. The dull environment shimmered, negativity flipped off like a switch. She was enveloped in warmth, hugged tightly by euphoria. Her eyes closed and her mind went blank.

She sat motionless for ten minutes before her brain let reality back in. Her buzz hadn't lasted as long as she had hoped for, and sobriety came back with a vengeance. When she started using years ago, she would soar for up to thirty minutes, followed by hours of pleasure. Now it hit her quickly, and left even quicker. It was never enough and she was already working out where her next fix would come from.

The stress from the fight with Jake took hold of her once more. She got up and went to the bedroom. She had to have more dope lying around somewhere, maybe forgotten in some hiding spot or spilled on her dresser. She just had to. No inch of her bedroom went unsearched, her hunt resembling a detective looking for evidence. Every empty drawer raised her anxiety. Lack of success weakened her physically. When she finished, her bedroom was in completely torn apart, covered with clothes, drawers, makeup bottles, papers and shoes. She was almost desperate enough to do the same to the rest of the apartment, but she restrained herself, knowing she never kept drugs outside of her bedroom.

She was once more on the floor crying. She felt defeated, not only in her search, but in every aspect of her life. Self-pity washed over her. She was twenty-eight, with no steady job and none on the horizon. Every ounce of energy she had went towards procuring heroin. She hadn't been fit to be a mother. Her son Gabriel was taken from her when he was only two. Another price her vice demanded. Her face was the epitome of ugly, tainted by a horrible scar with an even more horrible story behind it. She had no family, no friends – only fellow addicts who she kept around to avoid feeling alone in her plight. It didn't work. She had no responsibilities, assets, aspirations, goals, hobbies or interests.

I have nothing.

It wasn't entirely true. There was Jake, but he only stuck around out of habit and a sense that it was his duty to protect her. God knows she contributed nothing to their relationship and did nothing but hold him back from happiness. She hated herself for how she treated him, never showing appreciation. For years she had been a burden, nothing more. He was a saint for the way he cared about her. If she went on with her status quo, she would make him a martyr.

Her failure as a person choked her now, and despair took over. Any self-worth she felt was crushed. She didn't want to go on, couldn't even stomach the thought of another day. No one benefitted from her continued existence, and no one would suffer from her death. It would hurt Jake, but she would be doing him a favor in the long run by setting him free. It was the least she could do to reverse the harm she'd done to his life. She made up her mind right then. She wouldn't live to see tomorrow.

Faith grabbed her cell phone from the counter and sat on

the couch. Biting her nails, she scrolled through her contacts until she landed on Jake's name, then closed the phone. The thought of calling him made her anxious, but he deserved to hear her voice one last time, minus any threats. A note wouldn't do. She needed to get to his voicemail, where she could make her peace before he could try to intervene.

She continued to gnaw at her fingernails as she worked up the courage to make the call. There was a photo of them on her coffee table. She picked it up and held it on her lap. It hurt her to look at it, but her gaze was locked. The two were in a bar, smiling with drinks in their hands. Anyone else would have seen a happy couple, but she saw two fabricated expressions of joy. She remembered fighting with Jake earlier that night, before hooking up with friends. They were miserable the whole time, struggling to not telegraph the fact.

A tear dropped onto the glass, landing on Jake's face. He was handsome without the smugness that came with being jaw-dropping. Just right. His short, brown hair and muscular upper body made him look like a soldier.

She opened her phone again and called him. The anticipation was agonizing as one ring passed, then two. Five rings would take her to his voicemail message. The third, fourth and fifth passed, then, after a long pause, her own voice spoke to her.

"Hola! You've reached Jake, or actually, you've tried to reach Jake but didn't. Sorry! He's off in Oz dancing with munchkins on The Yellow Brick Road right now. Or he's shaving or something boring like that. Either way, leave him a message!"

Beep!

She hesitated, not knowing what to say or how to start. "I'm glad you didn't pick up, I was sure you wouldn't," she said finally, closing her eyes. "I want to say this and I don't want you interrupting me or trying to stop me. I don't want to fight anymore. And as long as I'm in your life, we'll be fighting, 'cause you know I'm never gonna get clean. I'm a prisoner for life, and you're too good to be locked up with me." She got choked up and had to take a deep breath before continuing. Her crying made it difficult to talk evenly.

"I'm a fuck-up. I'll always be a fuck-up. I can't imagine being anything else." Her own face in the picture stared back at her with a grin, as if amused at her self-evaluation. She hurled the frame across the room, where it smashed against the corner of her desk.

"I'm trying to say I wanna die. I need to be done. And this …" she struggled to get the next sentence out. "This … this isn't a scheme to get sympathy from you or a way to make you feel like a jerk. You've been perfect. Always. And I've been a disease. I'm going to die tonight, and this is my goodbye. I'm sorry I have to deliver it through a voicemail message, but I couldn't give you the chance to talk me out of it. It wouldn't have worked anyway, and you would have had to go through the rest of your life knowing that your last chance to save me failed. This way is better. Please don't hate me. Please don't remember me like this. And don't try to find me. I love you Jake, I'm sorry I stole your life. I'm sorry I was a—" A beep cut her off, signaling the end of the time limit.

"Junkie bitch," she finished.

Her mind was spinning at the thought of taking her own life. She hated the idea, despised it, but was uncontrollably married to it. With her last obligation in life completed, her mind tackled the tough decision she now had to make. She was terrified of every method she could think of. She didn't want pain, didn't want a mess. There was only one way she could accept.

Jake would head straight there when he heard the message, so she acted quickly, grabbing her phone, keys and pocketbook. She took one last look at her apartment, where she had resided for the past five years. Beat up as it was, she loved it and the thought of never seeing it again pained her.

She hurried out the door, not bothering to lock it. If the door was locked when Jake came, he'd kick it down in fear of her life. He had always had a key, but she'd been forced to change the lock recently when some drunk imbecile broke in. He was a former neighbor who entered the wrong building at two o'clock in the morning and mistook her apartment for his. When his key didn't work, he resorted to more extreme tactics.

As she turned from the door, a shape caught her eye. It was a young boy about ten years old, standing in the hallway staring at her. The sight was so odd, creepy even, that she could do nothing but stare back. He was a cute kid, dressed in a Spiderman t-shirt and carrying a backpack. His blonde, spiked hair made her think of her son Gabriel, who was also blonde and would be about the boy's age.

In the twenty years she had known Jake, they had been together for ten. They started dating at sixteen and had broken up for two years, starting when they were twenty. Gabriel was the reason for the split. More specifically, it was her pregnancy with him. She had made a stupid mistake in sleeping with another man – boy, rather – who she barely knew and hadn't seen since. She had no excuse for this, and never tried to justify it. The infidelity had left her pregnant. With the desire to be open and honest, she confessed to Jake that the child may not be his.

He stayed with her, but made it clear that he wouldn't be able to swallow not being the baby's father. The next nine months were trying. Both of them invested all of their emotions on the question of paternity; it made them tense. Jake still supported her, even with his uncertainty. He accompanied her to doctor's appointments and took care of her when she was sick. When Gabriel was born, they immediately did a DNA test and were both mortified to learn that Jake wasn't the father. He withdrew from Faith, barely speaking a word to her for two years. That period had been the genesis of her downfall.

The blonde boy in the hall made her sorry that she would never get to see her son again. After a second or two of silence, she turned away from the kid and made her way out, deciding that she didn't have the time to find out his story. He didn't seem to be in any kind of trouble, but her conscience still twitched a bit as she left him behind. She hurried down two flights of stairs and out into the parking lot. As she opened the door to her truck – a rusted excuse of a vehicle – she found herself being heckled by a neighbor returning home.

"Tell me something Faith," the man said with a large paper shopping bag cradled in his arms. He was a fat, disgusting man that lived a few doors down from her. "Do you enjoy putting your personal shit out there for the whole complex to hear?" He had a smug grin on his face like he had said something clever.

Douchebag.

"Mind your own business," she snapped back at him, stepping away from her truck and in his direction. She had always hated the man. He was a slob who felt it was his duty to express his opinion every chance he got.

"When I can hear your bullshit from four apartments away, it *is* my business," he said back to her, pointing an accusational finger at her from underneath the bag.

"If you didn't like my 'bullshit,' then you should've talked to the property managers or moved," she spat back while walking toward him. The man would be lucky if he got through this encounter without being kicked in the balls for his nosiness.

"Oh, you can bet your ass I'm going to talk to the managers, and I'll be the hero of the complex for doing it. Everyone here is sick and tired of hearing you and your boyfriend fight every other damn day." Faith could see that he was a bit surprised at her aggressive approach. It was satisfying.

"Well you won't have to hear it anymore. I'm never coming back to this fucking cesspool." For this, she was thankful. Since she moved in there, she had been treated as a pariah. In all fairness, it was her own doing, but it still killed her to pass neighbors knowing what they must think of her. She turned away from the man and headed back toward the truck. She had a job to take care of.

"And thank God for that," he called after her. "No one'll miss you, trust me." That stung.

"Feeling's mutual, prick," she retorted, then entered the truck. She started it and flew out of the parking lot like a prisoner being set free.

The highway zipped by her as she headed to the home of one of her dealers. His name was Paul Wilcox and simply put, he was an asshole. Unfortunately, he was the only one that decided to answer her call. He gained notoriety in the Orange District by ignoring decency and screwing over anyone who gave him an opening. The only reason she purchased from him was that he was a simple and reliable contact if you needed small amounts. Large purchases through him were only done by those who didn't know better.

If this deed of hers needed to be done – and her mind was still set on it – an overdose would suit her best. The plan hinged on Paul fronting her a bag, which wasn't a sure thing. She was a consistent customer though, and hoped that would give her leverage. Of course she wouldn't ever have to pay him back, and the thought of screwing him over for even a tiny amount gave her pleasure.

She was traveling in the rickety pickup truck that she despised bitterly. It had been her father's and it was given to her by her mother when he died. If she had any options whatsoever she wouldn't be caught dead in it. It put the image of that disgusting fuck into her head every time she sat in it, an image that twisted her stomach. While alive, her father's sole mission in life was to break her down. Her stories of beatings and verbal assaults could fill a library. He was gone now, but he had left remnants of himself in her life that taunted her every day. The truck was one. The ghastly scar that spanned her face was another.

Receiving that scar was the worst moment of her life. She had never known fear like she had when that monster grabbed her with a straight razor in his hand. She was only seven when he cut her. There were a few reasons he did this, none of them justifiable. The first was because, quite simply, he was crazy. He was a walking grenade and should have had a warning label glued to his forehead. The second was that he was stoned on crystal meth, which multiplied his craziness, spawning a downright wretched beast.

The third reason, and the one that was directly responsible for the scar, was that he had been fighting with Faith's mother. During the brawl, a violently demented idea crossed his mind. As a way of threatening Faith's mother, he decided that he was going carve into the poor seven-year-old's forehead. The two females of the family were spitting images of each other, and in a drug-fueled rage, her father had yelled, "Keep it up bitch, and this is what's going to happen to your pretty fucking face!" As he screamed the word "face," he slashed Faith and stormed out of the house without even witnessing the damage he had done.

As bad as this was, her mother took him back before the stitches came out. He never apologized, never even took notice of the wound. Up to the day he died he hadn't ever acknowledged the scar's existence.

When Faith became pregnant with Gabriel, she was filled with aspirations of showing him the love she never got. She wanted to be someone he looked up to and cherished. Instead, she fucked up and he was taken away from her forever. He was only two when Child Protective Services got tipped off that she was a heroin addict. She wished she could deny that she was, but it was true. Jake wasn't around for a long time to be her armor, and her life during his absence became a terrible mosaic of heroin, sex and sketchy acquaintances. She had ignored orders to go to court, a mistake that led to her ignoring orders to give Gabriel up. Eventually the police came and took him while she stood by helplessly. Appealing the decision was fruitless.

For years she cried at the thought of her baby growing up calling someone else "Mom." She would give anything to have known what he was doing right then. She had always wanted to send a letter, to try to reconnect in any way possible. A couple weeks ago she had finally gathered the strength to write one. She had to submit the letter to CPS since she wasn't allowed to know where he lived. She never knew if he got it, or even if his guardians did. It wasn't surprising when no answer came. And now there was no hope for a reunion with him.

She let out a heavy sigh as she took the exit for the Orange District. It was the worst part of the city, but she always felt comfortable when she went back there. Maybe it was because it was one of the few places she wasn't the most lost cause. She blended in there, which hurt her pride but unburdened her at the same time. Her comfort there didn't take away the fact that it was downright dangerous for anyone, let alone a young female, and to keep moving was always the highest priority.

It occurred to her suddenly that Jake hadn't called her back after she left the message. Did he get it? Maybe he called and she missed the vibration of her phone. She checked it and saw that she did indeed miss his call. *Probably rang while that fat fuck was budging into my life*, she thought, then played the message.

"Faith, if this is some kind of game, it's not funny. Please call me back. If you're serious, then you need to know that this is not the answer. Please … please call me back before you do anything you'll regret. I love you. If this is because of what I said earlier, I was just angry. You know how we get. Please Faith, you have to talk to me. Please. I couldn't … just … I love you. For Christ's sake don't do this."

What hurt her the most was the amount of times he said "please" during the message. His desperation made her wish she could console him. The message brought her even lower. She wanted to put the pedal to the floor and aim for the nearest wall, to finish it now. Survival scared her though, she didn't want to emerge from the crash a paraplegic or brain-dead. No, she had to stick with her plan. She clenched her teeth in an attempt to hold back more tears. They came anyway.

She closed the phone as she pulled up to Paul's house, which had to be the most poorly thought out exterior design ever. Its yellow and mint green pastel palette gave it the look of an Easter egg. Jake had gotten a kick out of it the first time he saw it, and for good reason. She didn't dare bring up the unfortunate facade to Paul, however. His sense of humor was nonexistent. She parked along the street right in front of the house.

This was it. Everything depended on the next five minutes. If all went well, she'd be free within the hour. If it didn't … well, she'd just have to cross that bridge when it came.

MAIN ROOM
6 7

OFFICE

POOL TABLES

BAR

KITCHEN

STREET

Jake's Discovery

Jake climbed back in his car outside Faith's apartment building. His next stop was Paul's house, which was the best lead he had to go on in his search for Faith. He pulled out his GPS navigation. He'd been to Paul's house a couple times, but wasn't sure exactly where it was, since Faith always drove. It was in the Orange District, which had a reputation of, among other things, being a maze for outsiders. What he *did* know was that Paul's place was in the same area as some dive bar called Husky Harry's.

Stupid fucking name for a bar, he thought as he plugged it into the GPS unit. *Wouldn't be caught dead in a place like that.* If he could get to the bar, he knew he could get to Paul's. Not that he wanted to. Only a situation as desperate as his current one would lead him there alone.

Paul was a massive piece of shit that peddled heroin to whoever was willing to throw money at him. Children, parents, addicts who looked like one more bump would be their last. No one was turned down. He had no morals when it came to getting his product into the hands of customers. No morals whatsoever for that matter. And money wasn't the only payment he would accept.

He'd gladly take TVs, jewelry, cars and any other trade he knew was in his favor. And of course the people who needed what he was selling would have no problem screwing themselves on a deal if it meant warding off their sickness a little longer. Jake heard a story of a fiend trading his two-year-old Chevy truck for what amounted to a thousand dollars worth of heroin. It was disgusting.

No doubt Paul took sexual payments too, the slimy fuck. Jake shuddered at the thought of Faith being so desperate. That suspicion had always lurked in the back of his mind, as much as he hated to admit it. If he ever found that out for sure, he would have killed her himself. There was no question Paul would have eagerly accepted a round in the sack with Faith in exchange for a bag. He probably hoped she *would* show up broke and desperate. Jake had seen the way he looked at her with x-ray eyes. She was gorgeous, after all, even though her former, sober self would have put her current self to shame.

Jake was embarrassed to think that he had told her that. It was rotten, raw emotions brought out during an argument. It seemed that all of his most shameful moments came about under those circumstances.

"Look at what that shit has done to you, Faith!" he remembered yelling at her once, after walking in on her with a spoon ready. It was the single most painful image he'd ever encountered. His reaction was based more on fear and hopelessness than anger toward her. "You look like shit! You're face is sunken in, you always have bags under your eyes. I'm embarrassed to even be with you. I can't even bring you over my mother's without knowing she's thinking terrible things." He wanted to cry now, thinking back to it. His cruelty was astonishing. It wasn't like him.

"You think I don't fucking know that?" she had yelled back with tears forming in her eyes. "It hurts me too. Everywhere I go, I know people are whispering, 'Oh, would you look at that strung out skinny bitch. Look at her arms, they're full of dots.' That's my reality. You think its fucking fun being like this? You think this is everything I ever wanted?" She buried her face into a pillow and sobbed.

"Then why the fuck do you keep doing this shit?" He threw up his arms, perplexed. "Y'know what? Never mind. Nothing you could ever say would make me understand this retarded bullshit."

He didn't give her a chance on that occasion to attempt to explain why she kept doing her drugs. The topic often came up, though, and there was another conversation they had that he never forgot. It was much more civil and calm.

"I can't justify what led up to the point where I'm at," she said, laying on her bed stroking her stuffed polar bear. "But I'm at where I'm at, and I'm stuck here. The physical addiction is only half of it, ya know. I live my life constantly accommodating my addiction. It's part of who I am. It's part of my personality. I feel like it *is* my personality. And that just makes me feel like even more of loser. The fact that it makes up that much of my being is the reason I can't stop. It's part of Faith. Imagine you trying to quit being Jake. Trying to quit enjoying books or liking sports, ya know? Imagine someone who writes every single day, their life based around putting words on a page. Then imagine telling them that they need to give it up forever. Now, I know writing and getting high aren't the same, but they can both rule someone's life to the point where their absence is devastating."

"But you could be so much more," he said. "The difference

between you and a writer is that a writer without writing loses something precious. An addict without heroin *gains* something precious. The addiction doesn't have to define you. You wouldn't cease to exist without it, you would become a better Faith. As corny as that sounds, it's true."

"It doesn't *have* to define me, but it does. This has been my life for years. Every day is the same shit. I wouldn't know how to live any other way. And this is just the mental addiction we're talking about. The physical addiction is a whole 'nother monster. Sometimes the sickness is so strong that I'd rather die than go without scoring."

Apparently that's not the only thing that triggers those feelings, Jake thought, remembering the conversation. He knew he was close when he passed Husky Harry's. It was a scummy-looking rat hole. In fact, the whole neighborhood reeked of shit. Jake felt like he could catch chlamydia just from hopping out the window of his broken car door. He never came to this part of the city willingly. It wasn't fear that kept him away, it was repulsion.

He knew the house was only a couple turns away. He'd know it instantly when he saw it, too. It was an ugly mint green house with yellow shutters. Jake would never forget that. He remembered laughing hysterically when he found out that the infamous drug dealer Paul Wilcox lived in such a terribly ugly abode. Faith warned him sternly not to let Paul catch him doing so, but that went without saying.

Once he was on Paul's street, he kept an eye out on the left side, scanning for the green abomination. Since entering the Orange District, he had spotted a dead cat, six homeless people, a child of about eight wandering, five hookers (approximately three of them actually females) and twelve liquor stores.

It's like I'm trapped in a ghetto constructed by Hollywood.

He finally pulled up in front of his destination. The house was contrasted by a gorgeous red Lotus Esprit and a white Land Rover in the driveway. The grimy fuck had good taste. Jake didn't want to give himself time to change his mind, so he marched right up to the door and knocked. He could hear yelling inside. He was half hopeful and half worried at what it could mean.

A few seconds later, a pale, bald man answered the door. It wasn't Paul.

"Can I help you?" the man asked rudely, clearly anxious to get back to whatever was going on in the house.

"I need to speak with Paul," Jake said. He tried to be stern, yet nonconfrontational. The declaration ended up sounding like a nervous plea.

"Paul's a little busy right now, come back later." The man started to close the door. Jake stopped it, provoking an irritated glare from him.

"Just let him know it's Jake, Faith's boyfriend." He hoped it would mean something.

"You're Faith's boyfriend?" He had a sudden spark in his eyes. "Well, Paul will definitely want to talk to you." He let Jake in as if those words were a secret passphrase.

"Has she been here recently?" Jake asked hopefully.

"She's been here, alright. Sit on the couch, Paul might be a little bit."

"When was she here? How long ago?" Jake was desperate for answers.

"Just sit down," the man said, pointing harshly at the couch.

His tone of voice had taken a devious turn that made Jake nervous. He sat on the couch as he was told. He didn't think he had a choice at this point. Heading for the door would've probably have gotten him into trouble.

The living room was filthy. Paul evidently had a strange obsession with newspapers, since there were at least a few hundred from various publications stacked in piles around the room.

Strange interest for a drug dealer, Jake thought, perplexed.

That day's issue topped off a stack of about a dozen next to Jake on the couch. The front page headline read, "The Teardrop Vigilante Strikes Again: Accused Child Killer Found Dead." It wasn't the first time Jake had heard of the vigilante. He'd been in the news sporadically in the recent past. Jake thought it was great. He wished he had the nerve to go around wiping out all the grime that this world gave birth to. He'd probably start with Paul.

"Yo Paul, we got a visitor!" the pale man called from the living room, quite pleased with himself for delivering such good news.

"Who the fuck is it?" Paul yelled irritably from another room. Jake could hear water running in a sink.

"It's Faith's boyfriend, bro."

The water stopped instantly. That couldn't be good. Jake could hear Paul's boots stomping quickly toward the living room. He stormed in with a crazed look on his face. He was an incredibly intimidating person, about six and a half feet tall with a bald head and thick beard. He wasn't wearing a shirt and his dozens of tattoos were visible, the most eye-catching one being a self portrait of himself as a zombie that took up half his chest. He was holding a wet, blood-stained towel over his left arm, which left a trail of pink water behind him. There was a black pistol tucked into his jeans, which was clearly visible due to his lack of a shirt. Jake knew he had stepped into a horrible situation.

"Where's Faith?" Paul asked furiously.

It was now clear to Jake why the pale guy was so happy to learn who he was. Whatever happened here, Faith was the cause. At least she was still alive, or was a short time ago.

"I have no idea, I swear!" Jake said. "I came here looking for her. If she did some—"

"She *did* do something," Paul said intensely, then removed the bloody towel from his arm. Underneath was what appeared to be a bullet hole in his bicep. "And you're gonna get that cunt back here right now."

"Fuck you, don't you fucking dare call her a cunt!" Jake said, terrified but trying to sound bold. He quickly found out that it wasn't only a useless thing to say, but an incredibly stupid one was well.

Paul's lackey grabbed Jake by the back of the neck and pulled him up off the couch. He kneed him in the stomach to hunch him over, then rammed him head-first into the corner of a wood table. Before Jake could even process the pain he was in, he was pulled up from the ground, kneed once again and shoved back onto the couch. He wouldn't be talking back again.

Paul pulled the pistol from his waist and kneeled down so that he was face-to-face with Jake.

"You obviously don't know how this works you little twit. I can call Faith a cunt if I fucking feel like it, because I'm in the position of power right now," he said, wincing subtly from his wound. "I can call *her* a cunt, *your mother* a cunt, or *you* a cunt. You see, Jimmy, until you tell me where that bitch is, I'm going to continue to do whatever the fuck I want. And trust me Jimmy, you don't want me to do whatever the fuck I want."

Paul put the pistol between Jake's legs.

"Now call that cunt or I'm gonna make sure you never fuck her again." Jake firmly believed that Paul's threats to neuter him with a pistol were not to be taken lightly. Unfortunately, he wasn't in a position to ensure his own safety, since he didn't think Faith would answer his call.

"OK, OK, I'll call." Jake said, trying to not make any sudden movements. The last thing he wanted to do was make Paul edgy.

"Ah, you see? Now we're getting somewhere." Paul said, sarcastically pleased. "It's good when people listen to us, isn't it Leo?"

"It's good, boss. Real good," the pale man agreed.

Typical yes-man.

"You should trust Leo, he's a smart guy. Now which pocket is your phone in?" Paul asked.

"Uh … right, my right pocket."

"Pull it out slowly. Don't do anything that's gonna make my finger jumpy."

Jake pulled the phone out as cautiously as he could, worried that something as small as getting caught on a stitch in his jeans would leave him without his manhood. He unlocked the screen of the phone and found Faith's name in the contacts. He pressed the call button below the picture of her at the beach.

"Put it on speakerphone," Paul said sternly. Jake obeyed.

After eight rings, Faith's voicemail greeting played.

"Hey there! You've reached Faith, or actually, you've tried to reach Faith but didn't. Sorry! I'm off in Wonderland having a tea party with the Mad Hatter right now. Or I'm in the shower or something boring like that. Either way, leave me something good!"

The message was followed by a beep. Paul leaned toward the phone in Jake's hand.

"Faith, Faith, Faith," he said in mock disappointment, "that wasn't a very smart thing you did, sweetheart. I'm willing to forgive and forget if you just come on back here and return what's mine. If you do that, we're good. If you don't, well … I'm sure you noticed that this call is coming from your boyfriend Jimmy's phone. He's not in a good predicament right now, Faith. If you're not here in a half hour, I'm going to make sure the two of you never have children. Every half hour after that, he's losing a limb." Jake's heart dropped at this threat. "Don't fuck with me Faith. I promise neither of you will get hurt if you do the right thing. I always liked you, I'd rather not have to do anything extreme."

He nodded to Jake, telling him to end the call. He did, then placed the phone on the couch beside him.

"Well, I guess now we wait. You had some very bad timing coming here, my friend. Faith left with a whole lot of my dope not ten minutes ago. On top of that, the whore shot me in the arm with my own piece, which she also took. If I had to guess, I'd say she had a death wish pulling a stunt that crazy, how 'bout you?" He chuckled softly. "And then you come waltzing in here like I just ordered a bargaining chip from a catalog. Lucky me. Unlucky you."

They sat in silence and waited a bit for the phone to ring. The quiet in the room made Jake incredibly uneasy. He was anxious, scared, claustrophobic, wired and angry all at once. The atmosphere of the house only amplified these feelings. He could see dust particles in the day's last sun rays, which slipped in through a crack in the curtains. Both of his captives sat solemnly, exuding dominance. Paul took the towel off his arm to check the wound. Blood streamed down to his wrist immediately.

"Fuck. Hey Leo, grab me a new towel from the basement will ya? Not a white one this time."

"No problem, boss, but keep an eye on that one," Leo warned, motioning to Jake. "You should back up a few feet so he don't try to pull anything."

"He ain't gonna do shit," Paul responded in a cocky tone. "I'm sure he like his balls too much for that." Leo headed toward the basement door.

"Now, why were you looking for Faith here, huh?" Paul asked, turning to Jake with suspicious eyes. "What did she do to you that's got you driving your shiny new car into my dirty neck of the woods? She looked mighty distressed when she was here. Tell me, did you two have a falling—"

Paul was cut off mid-sentence by a vibration from Jake's phone. It stopped too quickly to have been a call. It was a text message.

"Well what do we have here? Could it be a message from our mutual friend?" He grabbed the phone. "It is. Let's see ..." He started to read the text message out loud. "'Can't talk or listen to voicemail you left. In trouble. Go to Husky Harry's. Please come. In Rain Room.' Bitch sure didn't make it too far before getting herself into trouble now, did she? I guess carrying a pistol and shitload of dope will attract attention."

Jake had to make a move now; they knew where Faith was. Then, as if the universe was finally giving Jake a break, Paul yelled, "Hey Leo, get up here!" He turned his head away from Jake as he said this, and in a moment of carelessness and excitement, he lifted the gun away from Jake's crotch. The gun was still aimed at him, but was no longer stabilized from being rested on the couch. Jake didn't let the opportunity slip by.

He quickly grabbed Paul's wrist and shoved it away. The gun went off with a loud bang. Jake didn't think he'd been hit, but adrenaline kept him from thinking about it much. With the gun cleared of his torso, he elbowed Paul in the nose twice in rapid succession.

"Fuck, you little ..." Paul grabbed Jake by the throat with his wounded arm, while the other still had a death grip on the gun. Jake's only hope was to get that gun away from him, but he was desperately holding on to Paul's wrist to keep it at bay. There was no way he could gain control in his current position. If he failed to turn the tables, Leo would be back and he'd be dead in seconds. He was still sitting on the couch, but now Paul was straddling him and successfully cutting off his air supply. Jake had no leverage.

He grabbed Paul's wounded arm and jammed his thumb into the open hole. Paul screamed in agony. Jake headbutted him, causing him to release his hold on the pistol and fall backwards off the couch.

The whole struggle took less than fifteen seconds, just quick enough for Jake to have the gun pointed at the basement door as Leo hurled himself through it.

"Hey boss, what's going—" He stopped when he realized what he had walked into. His eyes widened in disbelief. "Fuck. Again?"

"Get on the fucking couch now!" Jake yelled. He took Leo's advice to Paul and backed up so that neither of the men were closer than seven feet. He wouldn't be a victim of any quick thinking on their parts. Once Leo was sitting on the couch, Jake turned the gun towards Paul, who was on his back on the floor.

"Give me one good reason to let you live. One reason why this world wouldn't be far better off without you!" Jake had never felt power like this. A squeeze of his hand could end a life. He was high on control.

"You're fucking right the world would be better without me, but you're too much of fucking pussy to pull that trigger," Paul taunted. "You better just get the fuck out of here while you got the upper hand."

Jake wanted so badly to kill the prick. It would be an act of justice. The legal system would never give him his just desserts. They wouldn't avenge the hordes of lives ruined by this man. Jake knew a few personally, it wasn't just Faith.

One of Paul's biggest customers was a former friend of Faith's. Her name was Joanna and she was a mother of two adorable twin girls. The girls couldn't have been older than six when Joanna died of an overdose. They found her with the tourniquet still wrapped around her arm.

One of the girls knew enough to call 9-1-1. This is what she told the operator: "A snake bit my Mommy's arm and now she's sleeping. Please help her, sir. We tried to give her medicine to help, but the shot was already empty." He'd met the girls once. The thought of their pure innocence clashing with darkness like that was one of the most traumatic things Jake had ever heard of.

Another of Paul's customers was Ed, a college dropout who would steal anything from anyone to pay for a bump. He had even tried stealing video games from Jake – and was caught in the act. Ed's mother had died a few years earlier and her engagement ring was his father's most cherished treasure. Of course it wouldn't be much of a tragic anecdote if he didn't steal the ring; he did.

Ed's father hung himself when he found out what happened.

Jake didn't think it was the loss of the ring that caused his decision to exit the stage. It was just an item after all. No, Jake had a hunch that it was the feeling of failure his father felt from having raised a creature with complete disregard to even the most sacred of things.

A few weeks later, cops responded to a call saying that there was a crazy person in the park yelling nonsense. They arrived to find Ed surrounded by a crowd of onlookers trying to get a glimpse of a complete maniac.

In front of men, women and children, Ed pulled out a knife and plunged it into his own chest. The scene had become legend in their city. Most thought it was Ed's father's suicide that prompted his, but Jake knew it was the feeling of failure he felt from being a terrible creature with complete disregard to even the most sacred of things.

Of course Paul wasn't directly responsible for these tragedies. Jake knew that. He was just the supplier. Chances were, Joanna, Ed and Faith would just hunt down new sources if Paul wasn't the scumbag he was. However, the world *would* be just a tiny bit better without him in it. Even so, Jake just couldn't bring himself to be world's justice.

"You're a piece of shit," he said, pointing the gun at Paul like an accusing finger. "You go through life not even slightly concerned about all the people and families you help ruin. You have no right to live, but luckily for you, it's not up to me to decide that. Next time you feel like a fucking hotshot who's above everything, just remember that you should be dead, and you're only breathing because I spared your pathetic existence." Jake lowered the gun, prepared to leave.

"I ain't remembering shit you pissant little—"

Bang! Paul's head jerked backwards in a spray of blood and whacked the floor.

Jake stood there for five seconds – gun smoking and pointed at Paul – taking it in. Then he turned his attention toward Leo.

"And you …" he started to say.

"Please man, I'm a good person. I'm nothing like Paul. Please don't do me like that." His eyes were wide with terror. He grabbed hold of the couch cushions, bracing himself for the end.

"Fair enough," Jake said, fully believing him. Leo wasn't evil, just a pathetic follower.

He started to walk out.

No, not yet.

He turned suddenly, aimed the gun back at Paul's lifeless body, and put one more bullet in his face for good measure. Then he left without a single blemish on his conscience.

If he had felt the need to defend his actions, he would have argued that he'd probably saved lives by taking one. Or that there would be less drugs in the city for a short while until someone picked up Paul's torch. Plus, he and Faith were safe from him now. But in his mind, there was nothing to defend. Nothing to feel remorse for.

He put the gun in his belt and bolted out of the house. A couple neighbors were outside of their homes, no doubt trying to glimpse where the gunshot had come from. If it was anyone else's house Jake had come running out of with a gun, onlookers would certainly have called the cops. But it was the neighborhood drug peddler's after all, and they were all most likely hoping that Paul's reign was done.

Jake jumped into the car and started it up. He floored it in the direction of Husky Harry's.

What kind of trouble has she gotten herself into in a place like that? Jake wondered. Then he realized that this was a suicidal runaway heroin addict who had shot and robbed a drug dealer less than an hour ago. He'd be surprised at this point if she could stay out of trouble. How did they get to this point? It was surreal to think of what he had done. It was even more surreal how little it bothered him.

He was at the bar within minutes, and didn't bother looking for a parking spot. He was still chock full of adrenaline and knew for a fact that the "trouble" Faith was in was urgent and couldn't wait for him to find proper parking. He pulled the Pontiac right in front and hopped out.

Inside, Jake found the bar mostly empty. The bartender was doing something behind the counter, only his head poking up over it. There were only a few scattered loners around, drinking quietly. It was a depressing scene. The walls of the bar were wood-panelled with black and white sports photos hanging arbitrarily every few feet. There were a few beat up pool tables in the rear of the place and some small dining tables. Smoke formed a cloud around the bar from the couple of smokers.

He walked straight up to the nearest customer, a distressed looking black woman at the bar.

"Excuse me," Jake said politely, but with urgency in his voice.

The woman turned to him, and he nearly jumped back in shock. She looked blank and deeply disturbed. Her hair was twisted and knotted, and hung over the right half of her face. She didn't respond, just looked intently at him. She struck him as completely crazy, as if her mind was taking a vacation. Then again, she could have just been hammered.

"Have you seen a blonde girl come through here?" he asked. "Late twenties with a long scar across her forehead."

"Haven't seen her," she said in a low, raspy voice, and turned away from him. Then, turning back toward him suddenly and excitedly, exclaimed, "*I* saw her." Her voice and demeanor changed. Her tone was soft now, her eyes focused.

"She went in the Rain Room with some man, just minutes ago. There it is, over there." She pointed to one of two doors at the back of the bar, past the group of pool tables. "But I bet it's locked."

"Thanks a—" Jake started to say before a loud gunshot rang out through the bar. Having just recently shot a gun, he was surprised by the volume of the blast. It seemed louder from a distance than his newly-acquired gun had sounded from two feet away.

The door to the Rain Room flew open and a burly, bearded man in an orange shirt ran out and left through the back exit of the bar. Before Jake realized what was going on, the bartender dashed from behind the bar counter and gave chase to the runner.

Then, out of nowhere, the woman he'd asked about Faith leapt to her feet, knocking him down in the process. She followed the two men out the back exit. The rest of the patrons were heading toward the front door in fear that the next gunshot would be the last thing they would ever hear. It was chaos.

Jake lay on the ground, stunned by the last ten seconds. He suddenly put two and two together and hopped up, making his way full-speed toward the Rain Room's door, which was still halfway open. He tripped as he was crossing into the doorway and fell forward onto the floor. When he looked up, he was horrified at what he saw.

Faith was laying on her back about five feet way from him, coughing up blood. He crawled frantically to her and held her head in his lap. She was covered in blood from the gunshot, which had opened up her stomach. She was hopelessly trying to cover the terrible wound with her hands. The woman he loved was dying in his arms. His worst fear was happening.

"Oh God, Faith. No, no, no," he cried. He grasped at his pockets desperately for his phone. He realized with a sudden horror that he had left it on Paul's couch.

Fuck, fuck, fuck, fuck, fuck! He couldn't believe his stupidity. The mistake could cost Faith her life.

"Someone call 9-1-1!" he screamed hysterically at the top of his lungs. "Please, for Christ's sake, call 9-1-1! Anyone!" No one answered. They were alone in the bar.

He sobbed and dropped his head so that it was touching Faith's. She let go of her stomach and held his arm. The blood was warm on his skin.

"You're gonna be OK, you hear me? This is nothing," he lied, placing his hand firmly over the hole in her torso.

She shook her head calmly. She knew it was the end. She had a look of acceptance on her face.

"I'm … I'm so sorry," she whispered, concentrating intently on getting the words out, knowing she didn't have much longer. "I'm sorry I was a burden. Thank you for … thank you for loving me anyway. You …" She couldn't gather the strength to finish the sentence. Her mouth hung open and her eyes rolled back in her head. She twitched, then her body went limp in Jake's lap. He let out a tired yell.

"No," he said, choking up between words, "you weren't. You

weren't a burden. You were everything to me. Please don't. Please God, don't do this to me."

He knew this was the end of the road. There was no life without her. He always hoped for a life with a sober Faith. He had always prepared for a life distanced from an addicted Faith. But never had he ever thought he could survive a life without her entirely. She was *his* addiction. Just like the writing to the writer or the heroin to the fiend. To lose her would be to lose himself.

He pulled Paul's gun from his belt and put the barrel to the side of his head. He was breathing heavily, trying to pump himself up for his trip to see her, wherever it may be. He prayed that all the religions who damned his last act had it wrong. He let out a deep, animalistic roar and pulled the trigger.

The last thought he had was of the day he met Faith. They were each playing in their own backyards, next door to each other. Jake snuck away from his parents to go talk to her.

"Cool scar," he said, as any eight-year-old boy would upon seeing such a sight. His innocence didn't let him wonder about what painful experience could have caused it.

"It's not cool," she responded, stopping the swing she was on. "It makes me ugly. Mommy bought me this pretty new dress, but everyone just sees my ugly face." She looked down ashamedly.

"I don't think you're ugly. You're the prettiest girl I ever saw, and your scar is awesome. I wish I had one just like it."

She giggled. "What's your name?"

"Jacob," he answered shyly, embarrassed by his name. "I like my nickname better. It's Jake. What's yours?"

"Faith," she answered proudly.

"That's a pretty name. Hey, you wanna play hide and seek?"

"Only if I get to hide first," she said.

"OK, I'll cover my eyes and count."

"No peeking! And you have to promise you won't go home and leave me out here. You *have* to try to find me," she demanded. Jake had a feeling that she had been left before. It seemed like such an odd request.

"You're silly. Of course I'll try to find you."

Gabe's Heartbreak

"Why can't you hear me!?" Gabe yelled through the bamboo bars of his handmade prison cell. He was in a jungle, scared, and hanging from a tree in a cage. He was sweating, partly from the heat, but primarily from his fear of heights. His cell was about fifteen feet off the ground, and the rope it hung from continued indefinitely up towards the canopy. The sky wasn't visible through it, and it was quite dark despite being daytime. The cage felt like it could plummet to the ground any second, its crisscrossing bars letting out cracking noises when he shifted too drastically.

Below him, two giant snakes were having a conversation. He could hear it, but his loudest screams weren't reaching them. They spoke as if he didn't exist, as if he wasn't suspended right above their heads. They circled each other as they conversed, never stopping for a moment.

"The boy is unpalatable, a cretinous creature more suitable for fodder than anything else," said the larger of the two, an orange monster speckled with green. The serpents were speaking English, so Gabe could understand their conversation, but found it impossible to keep up with their vocabulary. "A halfwit if I've ever seen one, and as frangible as a newborn. The pitiable little wretch is a terrible nuisance."

"I scourged it earlier, an expression of my disdain for its existence," said the other. This one was red, and though it was the smaller and weaker of the two, it was by far the more evil. It had the look of the devil, its eyes making promises of torture and pain with no words necessary. Gabe knew what it was referring to, despite not knowing what "scourge" and "disdain" meant. His back still stung from the incident it was talking about, and an occasional drop of blood ran down his back from the wounds.

"It's lucky it's too disgusting a specimen to eat." Gabe was terrified of what could happen next. He wanted his mother; a protector of any kind for that matter. None ever came though, regardless of how much he wished for it.

"We shall keep it in the cage until we can rid ourselves of it," said the orange one, with a flick of the tongue. Gabe did not know whether to be glad or frightened by this statement.

"We could just exterminate it," said the red devil, curling itself around the other. The two formed a knot, appearing to embrace each other. Their faces were inches apart, their eyes locked. "We'd do the world a favor. One less ignominious undesirable walking the planet. A defunct juvenile grows to a defunct adult unless it's cut down before it matures." The snake, which seemed to Gabe to be a female, turned towards him and raised itself off the ground. It rose until it was eye level with Gabe, then bared its fangs to him. "So effortlessly I could end you, little one. So effortlessly." He could feel her hate piercing him worse than her fangs could ever manage to.

The snake vanished suddenly to black smoke and slowly, the environment around him did the same. Solid objects became wisps of dark clouds. Everything broke apart and rose into the air leaf by leaf, stick by stick until all that was left was black. The nothingness of the scenery shocked him. Nonexistence was something to behold, and the emptiness tore its way into his emotions. His captors were gone, but so was the world. He didn't know where it had gone or if it would be back. His cage melted to a black tar and he fell through the soft bars, tumbling to the black ground beneath. The instant he hit it, he became part of the darkness. He too, no longer had solidarity. He lay there crying and alone, not being able to see a glimmer of light anywhere. He listened for signs of others, but only found silence. He wondered if anyone would ever come to rescue him; to show him happiness, to bring him out this empty darkness. He could only hope. And pray. And cry.

There on the ground he stayed, powerless, defeated and unable to bring himself to stand. He didn't think anyone would really come for him. This would be his resting place. To his surprise, he was relieved.

Bang!

The muffled but loud sound woke him abruptly. He scrambled to his feet, disoriented. He remembered that he had been in the back of his mother's pickup truck. He must have passed out. Wherever he was now, the truck was still. He was dizzy, which was normal after his episodes, but he fought through it. He looked around him. The truck was parked on the side of a street. It didn't look pretty; the houses were beat up and the road itself was marred with potholes. It wasn't like the pristine neighborhoods he frequented with the Jack and Allie. He turned to the cab of the pickup truck and saw the driver's seat empty.

I lost her, he thought in a panic. He got a grip on himself and realized that she must be coming back, he just had to wait.

Bang!

Another one, he thought. *What's making this noise?*

Gabe looked toward the direction of its origin. It seemed to have come from a green house across the street from him. He dropped down and peeked at the house from behind the wall of the truck bed. He waited in suspense for a few seconds and jumped when the door flew open to reveal his mother, who had dread written across her face. She was dashing toward the truck, a gun in one hand and some sort of package in the other. Gabe didn't know what to make of the gun or her frenzy.

He had been too paralyzed to hide from her, and she saw him now. She stopped in her tracks, and the two stared at each other for what Gabe felt was hours. He was completely unable to speak, and would have died if his life depended upon him doing so.

"What the hell are you doing in my truck, kid?" she asked harshly. She couldn't have remembered him from earlier, Gabe thought, since there wasn't an ounce of recognition in her face. She was on edge, her mind focused on something that wasn't him. He still couldn't speak, and his response to her question was a gaping mouth. The cruelty of her tone had hit him hard, which reinforced his silence. She didn't have to use the word "hell" with him. It was unnecessary. He hadn't wanted his mother's first words to him to hurt. Everything was ruined. A span of ten seconds had cracked the foundation of his beliefs concerning her. The veil was raised. In an instant she was no longer an angel; he didn't know what she was.

"Get outta there now," she said, and waited for a response. He gave none. "Now!"

Gabe was heartbroken at her treatment of him. He had daydreamed about the two of them meeting someday, and never had he thought it would be any less than loving and embracing. Would she have acted the same way toward him if she knew he was her son? He wasn't sure it mattered. She shouldn't have been that mean to anyone, let alone a kid. He was utterly crushed, and shuffled slowly and vacantly to the side of the truck and climbed out. Without another glance in her direction, he walked away, head down and crying.

This was why Jack and Allie had kept him from her. They were protecting him. His mother, his past – it was all poison, they had known it all along. He remembered all the times he'd asked them about her, all the questions. Their secretive, ambiguous responses made sense now. He wondered if his past – after her and before them – was equally poisonous. Perhaps they were protecting him from that, too. He didn't know what to think, his mind overflowing with doubt and uncertainty.

I never want to see her stupid face again, he thought to himself ten minutes later, about a half mile away. His short walk down the street had been grueling. With each step his body grew heavier and it felt as though his feet would give up and let him drop to the ground. He wished that Jack and Allie were there to take him home. He felt foolish. Even worse, he felt like a traitor for leaving them to find his mother. He had put all his hopes into meeting a woman who he didn't know. Her letter had painted a picture in his mind of a sweet, caring protector, but she was really just a witch. A witch who picked on kids and carried guns. She had passed him in the truck shortly after he began walking, and he doubted she even gave him a second look. She probably didn't even feel bad for him.

He had been kicking a soda can for a long time, but just now took notice that he was doing it. The can was quite destroyed, and Gabe wasn't sure whether it had already been that way or he had done it. Now he consciously took his frustrations out on the can, kicking it as hard as he could in the direction he was walking. It landed about twenty feet away and he was already looking forward to dishing out more damage to it. He caught up to it and gave it another whack, sending it into the road, where it was run over by a motorcycle. Gabe realized now how much he had been letting his mind drift The vehicle had been obnoxiously loud, yet it took the destruction of the can for him to notice it.

He walked on without his stress reliever, not knowing where he was or where he would end up. He knew the Morrisons' phone numbers by heart, so the only thing he needed was a phone. He prayed he wouldn't be forced to knock on strange doors asking to use one, but he would if it came down to it. He wasn't looking forward to explaining himself to Jack and Allie. He dreaded it, in fact, so he planned to walk until he couldn't anymore before calling them. He knew they would be disappointed with him. He hoped they wouldn't hate him and get rid of him.

He saw a police car ahead that had pulled over a driver. Gabe always felt anxious around police officers, yet he didn't know why. He'd always felt that way, and he certainly didn't want to be one when he grew up like all his friends did. He stared into the blue and white lights for a second and regretted it immediately. He blinked repeatedly and could only see spots. In his temporary blindness, he stubbed his toes on a rock that sat at the edge of a lawn. His shoes absorbed most of the blow, and he kept his balance, so no harm was done. He was now about a half of a football field away from the cop and the unlucky driver in front of him. As he neared the pair, he saw through his still spotty vision that the officer had the other driver out of their vehicle. He could hear them talking, but wasn't close enough to make out the words. He was only a couple of car lengths away when the spots finally decided to leave him. With his vision clear, he saw that the cop had pulled over the green truck that he had been hiding in just a short while ago.

The officer wasn't in uniform, despite having come from a police cruiser. He wore an orange shirt with an image of a motorcycle on the back and jeans. His clothes, plus his scruffy white beard reminded Gabe of Jack's friend Tim who always showed up on his Harley Davidson.

Gabe's mother was facing away from him. He hurried to get closer and hid behind a car parked alongside the street a few yards behind them. The cop was walking from her passenger door to where she was standing behind the truck. He could certainly hear them now, and was very curious to see how this played out.

"Why don't you go ahead and tell me what a little lady like yourself is doing with this," said the officer in a hostile manner. Gabe's view of the scene was limited to what was visible through the cruiser's back window and windshield, so he couldn't see what the officer was referring to. He assumed it was the gun.

"I found it up the street," his mother said dully, "I was on my way to turn it in just now." Gabe knew she was lying and he was only eleven, so surely the officer would see through it as well. This made her more of a villain in Gabe's mind. The gun had to be for bad things if she was lying to a cop about it. He'd seen plenty of movies where good guys had guns, and they never had to hide them or lie to police.

"Right, right. Of course" the officer said, faking belief. His demeanor then turned cold and harsh. "And I'm guessin' you just stumbled upon a boatload of dope too, didn't you? You're a lyin' little jezebel." Gabe didn't know what he meant by "dope." There was no one else around. "Do I have 'dumbass' written on my fuckin' forehead darlin'? Well I suppose I must. Why the fuck else would a dumb little bitch like yourself tell me some stupid shit like that?" Gabe knew this wasn't right, and he could feel his heart beating. Police shouldn't talk like that. They were supposed to be heroic, not vicious.

"You can believe whatever the fuck you wanna believe," his mother said defiantly. He heard a loud smack and saw her drop out of his view through the window. She yelled, "You have no right, you ugly son-of-a—" Another smack sounded loudly. He'd hit her. Gabe couldn't believe the cop actually hit her. However terrible she was, she didn't deserve that. He tried to get a better view, worried about her and wanting to see her condition.

"I have the right to do whatever the fuck I please, buttercup. Y'know why? 'Cause I'm a motherfuckin' officer of the law, and you're just a tramp who wouldn't be missed if I fucked you right here and left you dead in the street." Gabe looked around desperately for anyone who might be witnessing this. Around him was mostly factories and closed shops. The one house in sight didn't have a single light on throughout it. He began getting dizzy. It worried him.

Not here, he plead to his own body. *I've been out three times already today*. Gabe had never had so many episodes in such a short time. His adventure was weighing greatly on him, his body was overblown with emotions. The only time he'd ever fainted more than once in a single day was when the Morrisons had brought him to Disney World.

"Get up," said the officer, who was now walking around to the side of the cruiser. Gabe ducked back behind cover quickly. "Get in the back of the car. And don't try to fight it, 'cause if you play your cards right, I ain't even gonna bring you in to the station."

"If ... if we're not going to the station, why do I need to get in the back of the car?" Gabe's mother struggled to get the sentence out. He couldn't see her, but he could hear the desperation and confusion in her voice. His eyelids took on weight, his limbs weakened. He cursed his frailty.

"You need to get in the car 'cause otherwise you're lookin' at a whole lotta time in the pen with all them goodies you got," he said, opening the back door. Gabe's surroundings dimmed. "We're gonna take a ride, have a talk, and maybe if you're well behaved, I'll—"

Amy and Adrien's Agreement

Amy opened the door to the cab that would take her far away from the mess she was in. The driver made his way to the door, his hands full with convenience store purchases. He got in and struggled to get situated. He was a large man and the cab wasn't especially roomy. Watching him try to get himself all sorted out almost made Amy laugh out loud.

"So where am I delivering you to sweetie?" the driver said once he was comfortable and strapped in.

Amy planned to have him bring her to the train station, where she could further explore her options. Once there, she could buy the ticket that would put the most distance between her and Ron. Adrien apparently didn't agree with this plan. He pushed Amy aside in her own body and directed the driver.

"You know where Husky Harry's is?" he asked. "It's a dive bar in the Orange District." The request didn't vibe well with Amy's escape plan. She didn't know what Adrien was getting at.

"Know it?" the driver said excitedly, cracking open his bag of pretzels. "I'm good friends with the owner. He's a goofy bastard named Phil. Good guy. Real good guy."

"No shit. Small world. I know Phil too," Adrien responded, interested by the connection. Amy knew he was thinking something devious, and that made her concerned for the cab driver's life. "You happen to have a pen and paper up there?"

We need to get the hell out of this city, you moron. Amy thought to Adrien. *Why in the fucking world are you going to some shit hole bar in the Orange District? And I know for a fact that we don't know the motherfucking owner of that place. You lying to that man.* He remained silent.

The driver grabbed a pen and handed it to Adrien. Amy watched as her own hand wrote a message for her to read.

TWO MORE BEFORE LEAVING TOWN

Two more what? She asked him. *Kills? Goddammit Adrien, I put up with your shit constantly and I roll with the punches, but this is not the time to be a vigilante. We need to leave now. Ron has people all over this city. This fucking driver could be one of 'em. Who the fuck you need to kill that's so damn important?*

Adrien scribbled:

PHIL AT BAR. CAB DRIVER

WATCH FUCKING TONE WITH ME BITCH

What!? Why? Enough of this shit already. Adrien crumpled the paper and handed the pen back to the driver without responding to her. She knew she couldn't get control back anyway, so she didn't fight it.

After Adrien introduced himself to Amy by murdering her boyfriend, she was sent to a psychiatric hospital. It didn't surprise her, of course. To the outside world, she had just killed someone with a fork and blamed it on a demon.

"That boy you killed," Dr. Rick Moran said, sitting across from her at a white table, "what did he do to you? I'm sorry, what did he do to *Adrien*?" She had already told them all about Adrien. Of course they thought she was crazy or lying. God forbid they just believe her about her demon That would make her life too easy.

"He had GHB in his pack of cigs," she said, nervously rubbing the sleeve of her robe. "Adrien didn't care for that. I liked Nathan; a lot, I didn't wanna see him die, even though I was disappointed to see that on him."

"I know this is gonna hurt darling, but Nathan was innocent." He pushed his glasses up and studied her expression. "GHB isn't just used for date rape, it has legitimate purposes. It's commonly used for narcolepsy. He watched over his neighbor's son, who is a narcoleptic. It was Nathan's responsibility to give him his daily dose." He waited for a reaction to this news. He seemed disappointed when Amy gave none.

She spent many hours in a room with Dr. Moran, but never brought to his attention that she was being sexually abused during her stay at the hospital. It had happened three times since she had been in the thrown in there. It was an orderly. The son-of-a-bitch's name was Tim. He'd creep into her room after midnight with a needle full of wooziness. Amy was already strapped into her bed, so it was nothing for him to get a clean stab. Adrien was nowhere to be found during these visits. Not that he could've done a damn thing. She was strapped in and sedated. Completely defenseless.

Big man using restraints and drugs to get laid.

"You like that, you crazy bitch?" Tim would whisper while inside her. "Yeah, I'm gonna fuck you 'til you're sane again you pretty little whore." Amy never so much as a broke her blank countenance. She wouldn't give the pathetic fucker a bit of satisfaction if she could help it.

The act itself had very little affect on her. Every day she went out and slept with the nastiest, most vile men that her city had to offer. There wasn't anything some punk kid in his early twenties could do to her physically that she hadn't already seen and laughed at. She had knives put to her throat. She'd been beaten bloody and dropped in front of a hospital with broken ribs. She saw real menaces. She barely took notice while Tim was inside her, flopping around like an imbecile who had never had consensual sex.

But all that didn't take away the violation she felt every time her door got pushed open late at night. Those pestilent dirtbags she slept with for Ron paid for her survival. She didn't ever want to do it, but she always did it willingly. The ends justified the means. Tim went about his pathetic attempts at forceful sex as if he was entitled to it. Amy could smell the ego drifting off of him and could see apathy he had towards being a decent fucking human being.

She kept Dr. Moran in the dark about Tim's abuse. She held out hope that Adrien would show up and give the bastard what he had coming to him. She would endure his pitiful assaults until then. She fantasized about his death while he fucked her.

She talked about Tim and his nighttime visits to Sheila – a patient with an unknown mental disorder – during social time. Sheila never talked back. She never talked at all, actually, and Amy wasn't even sure she had anything going on inside her head. She vented to her nonetheless.

"He's the worst type of scum," she whispered, putting a jigsaw puzzle piece into place. "Too pussy to even give the woman a fighting chance. Coward." Sheila sat next to Amy at the table, her eyes fixated on the puzzle. She always had a look like she knew where all the pieces went, yet she never lifted a finger to help. " If I had a dick I'd rape *him* 'til he bled and cried for his slut mother. Don't you worry though, Sheila, Adrien will make sure he gets his. Adrien will come back eventually." It was all Amy had to look forward to.

She hadn't heard a peep from Adrien since the first night she was in there. He was a coward too. He knew he couldn't do a thing in that place, so he stayed away when she needed him the most. If he was there with her, maybe the doctors would see she wasn't crazy. Maybe he'd do something about Tim. Instead, she was alone to deal with the consequences of his violent whims. She had no choice but to wait in the hospital and deal with her situation.

"Amy," Dr. Moran said during one of their sessions, "have you ever considered that Adrien is *you*? What I mean is, could Adrien be parts of your personality manifested in an alter ego that committed a crime you yourself wanted to commit? And perhaps he is your way to keep a clean conscience for yourself?" He leaned back and bit the end of his pen.

Amy sat awkwardly across from him, staring at the table. She hated these sessions. She had been in the hospital for a month and she knew what Dr. Moran thought of Adrien. This was the first time he came out and asked it, but she knew. He'd been beating around the bush for weeks now, inquiring as to what Adrien sounded like, what he acted like. She had only talked to Adrien once at that point, and she had told the doctor all about it.

She told him how Adrien came through and spoke to her the first night in the hospital as she lay in bed. She was sedated, so she didn't remember the conversation verbatim. She knew the gist though, and that was enough to scare both her and her doctors. The only difference was that she was afraid of Adrien and the doctors were afraid of her.

Adrien had gloated to her that night about killing Nathan and ranted on and on about how scum like him deserved to die. He made it abundantly clear what his goal was. He was going to use her to dish out punishment.

She remembered being told that he was there to stay, and if she wanted to get rid of him, she would have to kill herself. He told her he was a demon trying to be an angel. That he had a falling out with the devil, and knew he could gain favor with God by killing those who did the devil's work. It was all very grandiose talk and Amy didn't know what to make of it. She was used to his speeches now, but at the time it was terrifying.

Dr. Moran inquired about Adrien's name. "Don't you think it's interesting that his name is that of your childhood dog? I'm sure you saw the dog as a sort of protector of you and your family. What if Adrien is simply your mind's way of securing itself and creating another protector."

Amy hated all the psychobabble. She fired back, "That ain't got nothing to do with nothing. There's millions of Adriens out there. You're trying to make connections that ain't there, doc. Adrien is *not* in my imagination. He's *not* an alter ego. He's a piece of shit that hijacked my head straight from hell and murdered my boyfriend!"

Amy felt a shameful rush when she agreed with Adrien's killing. Tim the orderly had been the first to waken this feeling in her.

Unfortunately for her, his nighttime visits became more frequent. Unfortunately for him, she noticed him becoming more careless. He apparently grew bored of the missionary position, which is all that Amy's restraints allowed him. He started unstrapping her legs in order to try new things. Over time, that led to one hand being set free. Amy had a few chances to try escaping, but she was too nervous. If she botched it, he'd put up his guard again. Instead, she was patient, knowing that his attention would continue to falter until she was presented with a golden opportunity. When that perfect chance did show its lovely head, it was not Amy, but Adrien who was there to capitalize on it. And that was the end of Tim.

She heard the lock of her door being turned. The sick sensation she was now conditioned to feel in response to that sound hit her hard. The door creaked open slowly. One thing Tim was always careful about was his silence. He threatened Amy in the beginning with death if she ever made a peep, even out of pleasure. As if she would ever get an ounce of it from his visits.

Arrogant fuck.

He strutted over to her bed as if he was the definition of swagger and dropped his pants. The second his belt hit the floor, Adrien's vacation ended. Amy couldn't have been happier.

Tim hadn't said a word since entering the room. His after-hours appearances were frequent enough now that no threats were needed, no taunts necessary. He always came in, did his thing and left, looking like he accomplished something that amounted to more than forcing his dick into a prisoner. It was disgusting, the way he always left the room with a smug grin on his face.

He unlocked her ankle straps quickly, as if this was some obligation he needed to get through quickly. Next, he freed her right wrist with the intention of turning her around and taking her from behind. Damned if Adrien was going to let that happen.

The instant Amy's wrist was free, Adrien used it to grab Tim by the back of the head. He yanked him close and aimed Amy's jaw directly for his Adam's apple, the same thing he targeted when he killed Nathan. Amy felt the blood stream down her chin and neck as her teeth sank deep and ripped out a fatally large chunk of Tim's throat. He gasped but couldn't make a sound beyond the thuds his spasming body made against the bed. Adrien grabbed Tim's testicles viciously and twisted them, then pulled his face close so that their eyes were an inch apart.

"Hope all that free pussy was worth it, you fucking cunt!" he said savagely, then pushed Tim off the bed to die wriggling on the floor. Amy relished the sight of it.

Adrien unstrapped her other wrist quickly and hopped on top of Tim's barely alive body. He frantically searched all of his pockets for a key. He was hoping to find the electronic card that would let him out the front door, but only found a ring of keys that controlled interior doors and the windows in the social room. Amy prepared herself mentally for what that would mean. She had a feeling she would be jumping soon.

"Fuck!" Adrien spewed in a hushed yell, knowing it too. He ran out of the room and down the dark hall to the social room. He made his way to the south window and started trying out every key on the ring. Out of about twenty keys, the one that finally spelled freedom for them was the eighth. It was a good thing too, because at the moment Adrien flung the window open, a commotion was being made back at Amy's room.

They were on the third floor, which meant that Amy would not come out of that drop with all her bones unharmed. Adrien didn't care one bit about the bodily harm that would come to her or her bones, so he jumped without a moment's hesitation. Truth be told, Amy would have eagerly jumped to freedom as well, but it would have been a far more difficult decision.

Adrien released his hold on her in mid-air, meaning she had no chance whatsoever to brace herself for the landing. She hit the ground in what resembled a belly flop and cried out in terrible pain. Once her mind caught up to the situation and she realized she was back in control and needed to run, adrenaline helped her along.

With nowhere else to go, she ended up at Ron's condo two hours later. When he opened the door, what he saw was his youngest money maker on her knees crying, soaked in enough blood to frighten a surgeon. She was terrified of what he would do to her. She was relieved when he showed mercy.

"Ho you better have an awesome muthafuckin' explanation as to your whereabouts and an even better one as to why you look like Carrie." He sighed. "Come on in, bitch. Come on in."

"So tell me cabbie," Adrien said to the cab driver, "what are your thoughts on death?"

"I don't know what your angle is princess, but that's some

awfully deep conversation to pass the time between here and that bar." He beeped at a woman in a minivan who cut him off. "Bitch."

"I despise small talk," Adrien said, putting Amy's hands behind his head and getting comfortable. "I'd rather explore someone's core beliefs instead of wasting time talking about the weather. So how 'bout you humor a gal and tell me your take on the subject."

"Well I imagine my views are pretty normal," the driver said, stopping at a light. He looked at Adrien through the rear-view mirror. "Death is just about the scariest thing out there. Only thing scarier than dying is the thought of dying painfully. Now, I guess if you're the religious type – which I ain't, not that I got a problem with all that – then death is a hopeful thing. Never understood how a religious person could be afraid of death. Ain't they supposed to look forward to heaven or something? Just saying. How 'bout you, darling? You seem like you're looking to get something off your chest."

"Well … I think humans put far too much importance on death. Life too, for that matter," Adrien said. Amy could tell he was just looking for an excuse to wax philosophical.

You're pathetic, this man don't wanna hear your stupid thoughts on the world, she thought to him.

He continued as if he hadn't noticed her jab. "There's seven billion people in the world and everyone treats each death as if it's some big tragedy. The only thing in life that matters is the continuation of a species. It doesn't matter for shit if an individual dies. The world will keep going. The universe will keep going. It's absolutely inconsequential." He leaned forward, speaking more intensely. "All that means anything is that humans as a whole stay alive. In fact, individuals living longer is going to bring the human species to a ruin. Think about it. People are living longer than ever with new scientific advances and the population just keeps getting bigger and bigger. You can take that as a victory on an individual level, but as a species it's going to be catastrophic. You won't be able to feed yourself soon. That's if humans even live long enough to get to that problem, with all the weapons they produce now.

"And that's just the start of it. People have no perspective when it comes to life and death, Americans especially. One fucking kid gets killed in a car accident or in the crossfire of a shooting and we throw around the word 'tragedy' immediately. Since I started this fucking rant, over a dozen children have died in Africa. That's no fucking exaggeration. Yet there's no news stories, no tweets, no Facebook posts. Nothing! But God forbid one child gets killed after being locked in an abandoned refrigerator in Middle America. All of a sudden you can't go anywhere near a water cooler without hearing how fucking sad it is. 'How tragic' they say. 'It's terrible.' Fuck that. The Holocaust was a tragedy. Slavery was a tragedy. Hiroshima and Nagasaki were tragedies. Some stupid kid getting himself killed is Darwinism, nothing more. At least those dumb fucks get to live decent lives in their short time here. There are places in this world where twenty thousand children die every day. And trust me cabbie, they did *not* spend their short lives at baseball games eating hot dogs or watching Saturday morning cartoons.

"And most people mourn the dead for selfish reasons anyway. Family members weep because they don't have their loved ones anymore. Like you said – if you did believe in Heaven, and you were sure that your dead grandmother was there, why the fuck would you be sad for her. You're either sad for you, or sad for others whose lives are affected by the death."

"You sound like you've been holding that in for some time there, girl," the driver said. "And I ain't gonna say you don't make a good point or two, but it's clear you ain't never had a child close to you die. If you had, you would never say that shit about it not being a tragedy. *Every* child's death is a tragedy, whether they died from Malaria in Africa or in a refrigerator in Middle America. Only reason no Americans make a fuss about the thousands dying elsewhere is because it's not shoved in our faces. It doesn't hit close to home. Guaranteed if those African kids were being shown on TV all the time and names were put to faces like them school shooting victims, people would see it a lot different. It's not peoples' faults, it's the media's."

Adrien responded somberly, surprising Amy, "What you said about losing a kid close to you – that sounded like a first-hand experience." This was the first time Amy had ever heard Adrien show anything resembling sympathy. It was odd, especially considering he was going to kill the man.

"Yup, my sister's husband and three-year-old son were killed in a car wreck. Drunk driver going the wrong direction on the highway. The stupid fuck hit them. Trust me when I tell you that it was more of a tragedy to her than any of those things you said, Hiroshima and whatnot. All I can do now is help her and my other nephew get by."

The three of them rode the rest of the way in silence. Amy was terrified for the driver. She didn't want to see Adrien kill him, not after knowing he was helping a family stay fed. The rest of the ride felt like a countdown. The driver pulled up in front of Husky Harry's and put the car in park.

"Here y'are," he said and looked back at her. "Now, because you're so pretty and such a good conversationalist, I'm gonna knock off half the price. I'm Marcus by the way."

"Adrien," Adrien said and handed Marcus half the tab, plus a few bucks tip, then got out of the car without incident.

"Now … I'm not complaining one bit, but what happened to killing the cab driver?" Amy asked Adrien, glad to be able to speak through her mouth again.

"I have my reasons for not doing it," he responded distant-ly.

"I'd call that reason 'mercy'. Interesting that you were ready to cut that man up until he gave you that sob story about his sister's family. I suppose God wouldn't much like that particular sinner wiped out? I never heard you be so nice to anyone. You even tipped him."

"Besides being pals with the shitbag who owns this fuck-ing bar, the man had no strikes against him," Adrien said. "God wouldn't be too fond of me killing off of speculation. Now shut your trap and lets do what we came to do."

"You mean what *you* came to do. And who the fuck is this Phil anyway? Of all the criminals in this damn city, why are you track-ing this random guy? We should be hightailing it out of here."

"You have the memory of an earthworm, woman. Remem-ber what Tricia told you? About the fucked up rape parlor Phil has going on in this bar? Figured you of all people would remember that, seeing as how it hits so close to home."

She did remember now. Her friend Tricia – another one of Ron's girls – had told her all about Phil and what he did to her.

"So I goes to that fucking bar, right," Tricia explained to Amy one night, "with a guy I met at a party. Danny something or other. I wish I remembered his last name now. Turns out he was a total friggin' douchebag." She took long drag from her cigarette. "The prick got to talking to Phil Harris, the owner of the dump, and told me to go pick a song in the jukebox like this is the fucking fifties or something. Anyway, I did. When I came back a minute later, Danny tells me he rented a room in the back of the bar. A private room that they call 'The Rain Room.' I should've left right then and there Amy, I swear. I thought it was weird that a bar was renting rooms out like a fucking motel, but I was too into the guy to make a fuss.

"So we grab some drinks and go into the room. We get to talking a little and we're making out when all of a sudden I start feeling woozy. I try to get up, but he just keeps kissing me. He's kissing my neck, my chest, nibbling on my ears and shit. Next thing I remember is waking up in the alley behind the place. He fucking raped me Amy, I know it. I felt dirty. My clothes were all fucked up like I'd been dressed by someone in a hurry." Amy covered her mouth with her hands. She was speechless.

"Yeah, I know, right? I still can't believe the shit. I swear I'd cut his fucking dick off if I ever saw him again." She took one last puff and put the cigarette out. "Then I got to thinking about it more and more. I know that guy Phil sold him the drugs that knocked me out. That's why Danny told me to go pick a song. I heard that place was sketchy. Now I know that cocksucker Phil's got a little scheme going. He sells drugs to assholes like Danny, then rents them the room to use 'em in. I went to my uncle who's a cop, but they can't do shit. Said there wasn't any evidence to convict him. And since I don't know Danny's last name, or shit else about him, they couldn't do nothing about him either."

Tricia had unknowingly increased her chance at justice by telling Amy the story.

She could feel Adrien bubbling with excitement as he prepared to enter Husky Harry's.

"I don't say this often," she told Adrien, "but I think I'm right there with you."

"That a girl. I knew you'd come around."

OFFIC

(5)

R.AIN ROOM (6)(7)

FIRE EXIT

POOL TABLE

(2)

(1)

STR

Ron's Machine

Ron was a genius, but also a complete piece of shit. He was self-aware, so he knew these two things to be true. His mind could have made him a leading physicist, doctor, engineer, writer or professor. Any field he chose, he would have excelled in. He mastered everything he tried from musical instruments to chess, without fail. He could have brought the world so much good.

He instead chose to excel in pimping, the one thing he could see himself doing forever. He wasn't ashamed of this and never looked at his unchased options with any feeling of loss or regret. On the contrary, he was quite proud to have honed his business skills to elevate a profession that was so lacking any smidgen of brilliance. He had taken a disorganized practice and spun it into a perfectly oiled machine. His machine sent over three dozen girls out into the city every day and night to satisfy lonely, adventurous or simply bored men. There were so many girls and they came from such different parts of the city that most didn't even know each other. The stable he commanded was of the highest quality, and no customer in his or her right mind dared to treat them wrong. Ron had a well-earned reputation. To fuck with one of his girls was to fuck with his money. And to fuck with his money was to commit suicide.

Ron's prosperity gave him the power to employ certain officers of the law, which not only dealt with violators, but also ensured the continued operation of his machine. Right now, however, there was a gear out of place in that machine fucking up the whole thing. And that gear's name was Amy.

Amy was a pretty little thing that had been with him since she was sixteen or seventeen. She had been a homeless orphan with nowhere to go, so he took her off the street and gave her a way to earn. He liked her a lot, but she had finally pushed his patience over the limit. Unfortunately for both of them, she had recently and quite puzzlingly taken up the habit of killing clients. He couldn't have bitches getting away with that. These were the people Ron depended on to keep a roof over his head. He couldn't think of a worse business practice than to let paying customers be killed by his employees. No intelligent business owner would stand for that. And besides, a dog that was rabid enough to kill those who feed it had to have something seriously tweaked in its head. The world would be safer if it was put down.

He was forgiving when she disappeared for months and showed up bloody and battered with a wild story of murder and psych hospitals. It was in his best interest to do so, after all, since she brought in enough money alone to cover his overhead. She was quite the earner. She had worked up such a prestige that he could charge double for clients asking for her specifically.

He had discovered her newest victim at one of his spots less than an hour ago. He remembered the poor bastard approaching him and requesting, "the sexy black bitch everyone is always talking about." That would be Amy. Of course the guy had also unknowingly requested a knife in the jugular. This was the second time Amy had done this to a client, and it would be the last.

Upon finding him, Ron immediately put the word out that he would pay good money for the bitch. His asset became a liability and that wasn't good.

It was nothing for him to kill such a business risk. Anyone or anything that was a danger to his empire had to be taken out, end of story. He'd killed plenty of times before; sometimes his girls, sometimes unruly clients.

He had a vast network of eyes and ears that could feed him any information he needed in an instant. Ten minutes after he put the call out, he was alerted by one of his girls that she was *with* Amy, playing pool in some hole-in-the-wall bar. Ten minutes. The efficiency surprised even him. Ron thought that the whore must have been truly cuckoo to be anywhere in this city after crossing him, let alone leisurely playing fucking pool. She sure had some nerve.

He thought back to the night she came to his door looking like something out of a horror movie, claiming to be possessed by a demon. Adrien, she called it. He didn't know what to think then, but he was seriously considering now that the bitch was a schizophrenic. He'd become knowledgeable on the subject during a brief, but very intense interest in mental disorders in his early twenties. He'd studied neurology and psychology purely out of curiosity, sometimes even sneaking into large university classrooms and listening to lectures. It was a habit of his to become so immersed in a subject of interest that he would focus on nothing else for weeks or months. He never attended college, but his comprehension could rival most undergrads majoring in their particular field. He was adept in criminology, biology, chemistry, classic and modern literature, botany, art history, business management, philosophy, music, information technology, engineering and anthropology. Beyond these, he had a basic understanding of an extraordinary number of topics. He credited his success in the prostitution business to his high regard for learning. Lack of education was what gave his profession a bad image. It had no respectable thought leaders raising the bar, just unorganized morons who were no better than the whores they commanded.

He knew that schizophrenics suffered from a wide variety of hallucinations and delusions, which could easily manifest themselves as a demon. He didn't consider himself qualified to diagnose this, but his money was on Amy being a schizo. She showed all the common signs: delusions, scattered thinking and speaking, paranoia and seclusion. Ron also considered all religion and supernatural beliefs to be nothing more than a crutch for the weak, so he saw the possibility that there actually *was* a demon named Adrien as out of the question.

This contemplating on the cause of Amy's actions did nothing to improve her fate, however. He was a logical man, not an emotional or sympathetic one. He wouldn't allow such deeds as hers go unpunished. Order had to be maintained in his stable, and that meant sending a strong message when a bitch fucked up. He couldn't think of a bigger fuck-up than skewering one of his clients.

He was en route to her location, a dump that some dumb fuck named Husky Harry's. He didn't need to be a whiz in business to know what horrible branding that was. He parked a few blocks away and walked, since his bright red Ferrari F-50 was far from subtle and he didn't have the time to grab one of his more indistinct vehicles. He didn't want Amy seeing (or hearing for that matter) his pride and joy pull up to the bar, nor did he want to be seen leaving in it.

Once there, he'd inconspicuously walk in, find her and treat her forgivingly. She had a timid and trusting disposition, so he knew it would be easy to convince her that he was on her side.

"We'll get you some help," he'd say, or, "I understand your problem." With her trust won, he'd take her to the side parking lot to talk about what they could do to help her situation and he'd put a bullet in her brain right there. It was dark now and he was dressed plainly, so he wasn't worried about being identified. He doubted the shit hole had any cameras, but he had little concern even if it did. He had already informed one of his police contacts about what he was doing, so any tracks he made would be covered. He'd leave the gun, which was given to him as payment for a night with one of his girls. It had no ties to him.

He was about two blocks away when he heard a muffled bang from up ahead.

Probably some two-bit crack dealer shooting a junkie for missing a payment, he thought. The Orange District disgusted him. There was filth everywhere – in the form of both people and garbage. Even as he walked, he had to watch his feet to make sure his clean, white sneakers didn't step in some unidentified substance. He didn't even like sending his girls to this part of town. The customers were mostly despicable and the girls always complained about their visits there.

Ron was fearless, but common sense made him watch his

surroundings very closely. There was at least one homicide every four days there, usually innocents caught in the middle of petty drug rivalries. Even with a piece on him, he knew his safety wasn't guaranteed.

He saw the bar ahead and noticed a couple people huddled around the entrance. He scanned their profiles, though he couldn't see them clearly from this far. He decided that none were Amy. He hurried his pace a bit, walking briskly for a block before hearing another bang, definitely a gunshot this time. It was close by, and sounded like it came from an alley beside his destination. Maybe he'd get lucky and find that someone else had done his dirty work for him.

A few seconds later, two more shots came from the alley. Ron pulled his pistol from his belt and pressed his back to the building beside the alley. As he peeked around the corner, his eyes were drawn to a young boy of about ten running panicked toward him. The kid was running for his life, there was no doubt about it. The horror on his face was not one of childhood imagination or exaggeration. It was very real and spoke of imminent danger.

Ron stepped from behind the wall to help the child.

⑤

RE
TT

RAIN ROOM   ⑥ ⑦   OFFICE

POOL TABLES

TABLES

BAR

STREET

Faith's Fight

Faith sat in her truck, anxiously staring at Paul's hideous house. *Here goes nothing.*

She got out of the vehicle, walked up the path and rang the doorbell. She was greeted by Leo, Paul's lackey whose sole purpose seemed to be acting like a generic henchman from a spy movie. He had no thoughts of his own, only what Paul put in his head. He was always sweet to her, but it was only because of what was between her legs; she wasn't fooled for a second.

"Hey girl," he said, eyeing her creepily. It got under her skin when he called her that. It got under her skin when he ran his gaze up her body. Everything he did, in fact, got under her skin. "Looking for Paul?"

"No, I'm looking for you," she said sarcastically. He probably took her sarcasm as flirtation, but she couldn't help teasing the poor bastard. He was just so pathetic. Her jab wasn't accompanied by her usually light mood, however, and he noticed. The search for death had apparently took the spark from her personality.

"What's got you down, girl? Needing a fix?"

"It's personal, asshole. And yes, I do. Where's Paul?" He put his hands up as if to shield himself from her hostility. Paul entered the room before Leo could respond. His presence demanded attention and any room he inhabited, he owned.

"Hey there Faith, what can I do for you?" he said with a fake smile. "Eh, who are we kidding? I can answer that for myself. How much do you need?" He lit a cigarette and waited for an answer. She realized then what she was to them: just another junky making a purchase. Maybe they were right.

"I need a gram and a half, and I was hoping I could pay you later today," she said with her head down, hopelessly dependent on his generosity. She wasn't optimistic.

"Whoa! That's a bit of dope you're asking for, sweetheart. You know that's three hundred bucks, right?" She nodded without a word. He thought for a few seconds while taking a drag from the cigarette. "I don't know, I'll think about it. Have a seat. You want a drink or something?"

Faith didn't want a seat or a drink; she wanted an answer. What was there to think about? It was a simple decision, especially for a man who could afford to burn grams just to heat his house. Unfortunately she was at his mercy, so she sat down.

"I'll take a water."

Paul looked at Leo. "Go get Faith a water, fool." Leo did as he was told, shaking his head subtly as he left. Faith looked around the room, which was filled with newspapers. She hadn't been there in a few weeks (she had other sources she'd rather call) and she was seeing the papers for the first time. It was a queer sight.

"What's with all the newspapers?" she asked, breaking a short silence.

He exhaled a cloud of smoke and grinned. "I might have done something bad a month or so ago. I might also be scanning the news to make sure it goes unnoticed." She knew the details would end there, so she didn't press him for any more information. She was probably better off not knowing; someone had most likely died over drugs. Paul made no effort to hide his brutality. Everyone knew he was dynamite with a lit wick. Even as they sat there, Faith could see a pistol on his waist under the t-shirt he wore. It sickened her. She must have telegraphed her feelings, because he chuckled a bit.

Leo came back with the water. Paul took it from him and asked him to give them a minute alone. Leo put up no fight. *That's a good little henchman*, Faith thought.

"You don't like what I do, do you Faith?" Paul asked her, smiling. He gestured to the pistol.

"I have no problem with what you do," she lied. It was unconvincing.

"No, I can see it. It's written all over that pretty face. You've been coming in here for a few years now, huh? You've seen things here. Heard things I've said. No doubt the rumor mill churns out fresh stories about me regularly. Tell me the truth. What do you think of me?"

"If you want the truth – and you asked for it, remember that – then I don't think you're a good person. I think you prey on the weak. You benefit from their misery." She found it impossible to meet his eyes as she critiqued him.

"And yet you need me." He put a finger under her chin and lifted her head up to meet his eyes. "Look, I just give the weak what they need. The fact that I profit from it makes no difference. If it wasn't me, they would go to someone else. You know that."

"But your way of doing business is unnecessarily rough," she said, gaining a little confidence.

"'My way of doing business'? What's that supposed to mean, Faith?"

"Like you just said, I've heard you say things. I've listened to that rumor mill. You don't have to quarrel with people. You don't have to sell drugs to mothers with starving infants at home. You can make your money and have a conscience too." She expected her analysis to anger him, but instead he laughed.

He leaned back in his chair and rested his right foot on his left knee. "You're living in a fantasy world, cupcake. Look around you. The world and the people in it are going to shit. That mother with the starving infant is an adult who can decide for her god-damned self if her money is gonna go into her veins or her child's stomach. I don't force these people to come to me. I don't advertise or have fucking sales to draw in customers. I simply sit here and make transactions.

"And why should I care about them anyway, huh?" He put his cigarette out in an ashtray on the coffee table. "I *was* that kid whose mother was on drugs. No one cared about me. No drug dealers ever refused her business on account of little Pauly. It's every man for himself out there, darling. The addict doesn't care for their kid, I don't care about the addict, the cops don't care about me, politicians don't care about the cops and the world doesn't care about politicians. It's apathy from the roaches all the way up to the gods. Humans are made to care about themselves. It's our instinct."

"You're wrong," she said, not quite able to back up the statement. She didn't even know if she believed it herself.

"Am I now? Do you live in the same world that I do?" He leaned forward in his chair. "Humans are an evil breed. Let's take you for example. Here you are looking for drugs from me, while your boyfriend ... what's his name, Jimmy?"

"Jake," she corrected him. She knew where this was going.

"Right, Jake. While Jake sits at home wishing he could get you to sober up. I've seen him the couple times you brought him along. He ain't down with this shit. And yet you put your own selfish, unhealthy self-deterioration before his feelings. To you it's just another day, but I'm sure his emotions take a beating every time you get high."

"But it's—"

"It's *not* different. Let me finish, there's a point to this rant, I promise. Now if Little Miss Morals can show that kind of apathy for her one true love's feelings, then just imagine the values you're gonna get from a regular Joe Schmo. Everybody in this world is rotten, Faith. Just to different degrees. You got preacher's touching kids, politicians taking bribes, students shooting schools, husbands murdering wives, mothers murdering children, addicts tearing apart families, men raping women, warlords terr—"

"That's enough!" she shouted, interrupting him. "I get it."

"Well that's good, I'm happy you get it." He smirked deviously. "I hope now you don't see me as a bad guy, but just someone who's looking out for his own interests. And I'm sorry to let you down, but it is *not* in my best interest to loan you that gram and a half. Since I'm such a bad guy and all, you're gonna have to either pay or go somewhere else."

She couldn't believe he was actually denying her this, after all the money she'd sent his way over the years.

"Please, Paul. I've been a loyal customer, there has to be something I can do."

"Loyal customer? That's a stretch. You know damn well you only come down to my neck of the woods when your other options are exhausted. And there's nothing you can do. Maybe if you were looking for a half a gram or something I'd let you pay me with some pussy." He grabbed her knee and squeezed it lightly. "But a quickie with you ain't worth no gram and a half."

She slapped him in the face, but the perfect blow barely made him flinch. "You're a sick fuck if you think I would stoop so low as to fuck you for drugs. I wouldn't fuck you if my life depended on it."

His demeanor switched to rage instantly. Her heart dropped at the sight of his new, vicious countenance. Without getting up from his chair, he grabbed her by the throat and pulled her face to his.

"I could make you prove that right now, you little slut. Slapping me like that, you must be looking for another scar across you're fucking face. You want me to make an 'X'? Huh bitch?" She was choking and grasping at his hands, but not even both of her arms could match the strength of one of his. "You think I'll lose sleep if I have to scan the newspapers for one more police discovery? You think anyone but your little puppy dog boyfriend would miss a junkie like you?" His grip on her throat was relentless.

He was going to kill her, she knew it. She should have welcomed it. It was death she was chasing, after all. And here it was, at her service.

Her mind suddenly cleared. As she was faced with demise, she realized its ugliness. The will to live that had been absent from her for so long took over now. In the span of a second, she thought of all the things she needed to make right. Jake. Gabriel. Her despicable past. She couldn't go out now, at such a low point. No end would be more empty.

She remembered the pistol tucked in Paul's pants. It was

her only chance, and that chance depended on the safety being off. She reached for it and after a second of fumbling for the handle, got a grip. She yanked it from his waist and pointed it at his chest. As she pulled the trigger, which was much tougher to do than she expected, Paul hit her hand aside. The gun went off and he howled in pain. She didn't know where the shot landed, but he jumped back in shock and his chair toppled over backwards. Faith sprung up from the couch and pointed the gun squarely at him as he rose from the floor.

Paul held his left bicep with his right hand and she could see blood leaking out from behind his fingers. His breathing was heavy and he stared at her maniacally.

"You fucking cunt! I'll have your fucking head for—"

"Shut the fuck up!" she yelled, and put her other hand on gun to steady it. "Or the next one is going in your fucking head." Leo came running back into the room, then stopped suddenly at the unexpected scene. The gun in Faith's hands made him put his arms up in surrender. "Leo, where's his dope? The big stuff, not fucking gram bags."

"It's in the floor vent," he said immediately, his eyes never leaving the barrel of the gun. "Behind you."

"Damnit Leo!" Paul said. The blood from his wound was everywhere now. His white shirt was now red and sticking to him.

Faith backed up, keeping her eyes and the gun trained on the two men. When she reached the wall, she bent down and removed the grill from the floor vent. There was a string attached to it that led down into the opening. She set the grill aside and pulled the string. About three feet of it came out before three bricks the size of tissue boxes emerged. She had never seen so much heroin in one place.

Surprisingly, she didn't feel any desire to take it for herself. Paul's words about her selfishness in addiction hit her hard, and the bricks looked to her like an animal baring its teeth. The feeling was new to her. It was exciting. She wanted to see the bricks burn, to destroy them before they could do more damage to anyone. She tucked the package under the arm holding the gun and reached for the front door with the other. She had officially crossed the point of no return. Her life would never be the same.

Paul stared at her with pure malice. "I'm gonna give you one chance to leave that on the floor and disappear, or I swear to God, I will kill everything you—"

Bang!

He was silenced by a gunshot aimed a foot over his head.

"I'm gonna give *you* one chance," Faith said, slightly buzzed on power, "to get down on your knees like the bitch you are. You too, Leo." They both did as they were told. Once down, Paul spit at her. He looked like a powerless dog still trying to show it's dominance. It was pitiful.

Faith opened the door behind her and left the house, soaring on adrenaline. She had never felt better in her life, but urgency dominated her mind. If she wanted to stay out of a cell or a coffin, she needed to pick her moves carefully. She sprinted the short distance to her truck and was stopped promptly by an unexpected discovery.

In the bed of her truck, staring timidly at her was a young boy. He looked familiar. Very familiar, in fact, but her mind was pirouetting far too fast to work out the mystery.

"What the hell are you doing in my truck, kid?" she blurted out, regretting her harsh phrasing. She was stuck in an aggressive groove, unable to switch gears. The kid made no response, just stood stone-faced. His eyes didn't leave hers for a second and she wondered if he had even noticed the gun in her hand and the bricks under her arm. She knew the neighbors would, especially if any had heard the shots and were now peeking out their windows. She didn't have time for kid gloves. She needed to get the boy out of her truck and then jet.

"Get outta there now," she said sternly. He made no movement whatsoever. "Now!" She didn't want to yell, but it was necessary at this point. It worked. He sullenly climbed out of the bed of the truck and walked away without a word. He had been so silent and melancholy that he had an air of an apparition. She gave it no more than a second of thought, and ripped the truck door open.

She threw her newly acquired items onto the passenger seat and drove off. The boy walked with his head down as she passed him. She was puzzled by his presence. Who was he and why did he look so familiar? Why was he in her truck bed? She wished she could get another look at him, but couldn't get a clear view as she drove by. She had a strong urge to go back and pick him up, to make sure he got home safely. There was a feeling of responsibility she felt to him that had no basis at all; it was just a gut feeling. She couldn't do that though, since she was now on the run. Plus, a truck with a gun and heroin in it wasn't fit for a child.

Her next move was a mystery to her. She drove away aimlessly There was a tenacious urge in her to disappear and start anew. She could sell the drugs and find a place far away. No, she couldn't possibly bring herself to peddle that poison. She wouldn't become Paul. She'd have to find another way out of the city. She could get clean, get a job in some distant place.

A life without drugs scared her. A life without Jake mortified her. He would never go with her. He had too much to sacrifice, whereas she had nothing. She couldn't stay, that was a definite. Paul would stop at nothing to find her and she needed to be far from his reach. This new prospect was terrifying, but it invigorated her as well. She was still riding the high she received from over-powering Paul, and had never felt more able to tackle life. Her first order of business was to destroy his stash.

Her thoughts had been jumping around so wildly that she didn't notice the blue and white lights flashing behind her. When she finally glanced at the rear-view mirror, her high vanished.

Gabe's Saviors

Gabe found himself sitting at a steel table in a cold, metallic room. There were no windows, the only connection to the outside world was a closed door with no handle. Across from him was a man who had never smiled in his life. Gabe was certain of this, but was clueless about how he came upon that certainty. He didn't know who this man was exactly, but was positive he was an enemy. He wore a black suit and sat with his arms crossed. There was no care or sympathy in his face.

"Someone's coming for you, kid," the man said matter-of-factly. "Someone to take you away." His voice was deep and monotonous. He spoke like a robot.

"Who are they? Where am I going?" Gabe squirmed with anxiety. He noticed that he was biting his bottom lip. He wondered if the squirming and lip biting was something he did regularly. He'd never caught himself doing it before.

"Who cares and who cares?" his rival said, answering both questions. "Could be Mr. and Mrs. Lollipop coming to take you off to Candyland. Could be Dracula taking you to some deep, dark cave. Hell, it could just be some fat slob nobodies bringing you back to a shack they call their home."

"I … I sure hope it's the Lollipops," Gabe said timidly. He thought that was a stupid thing to say, but the man's remark caught him off-guard and confused him.

"I hope it's Dracula," the suited man said flatly. The only emotion Gabe could read on his face was disgust. He didn't want to be in the room any more than Gabe did. He didn't want to help Gabe, or even look at him. "But as long as you're out of my hair, I guess I don't give a flying fuck who walks through that door to cart you off."

"Oh … OK," Gabe said. He sickened himself with his own cowardice, but felt completely impotent in the presence of the suited man. He felt as if he were up against Satan himself. "Why … why don't you like me, sir?"

"Why exactly *would* I like you, huh? You're a joke. A prank that life is playing on me. A lump of shit that was left on my doorstep in a flaming bag. And since stepping on you would ruin my good shoes, I figure the best thing to do is to scoop you up with a shovel and leave you on someone else's doorstep. And that person might step on you, get shit all in the treads of their sneakers. Or they might leave you on another doorstep. One thing's for certain though, no one will ever take the lump of flaming shit in. Not even the person who shit you out in the first place." He laughed and leaned back, crossing his legs. There was a cigar on the table beside an ashtray; he picked it up and lit it.

"How does it feel knowing no one wants you?" the man asked, then blew a cloud of smoke in Gabe's face, making him cough. "Not even your junkie whore of a mother. Cunt probably sold you for a ten minute high." Gabe jumped up suddenly and swung at the man. He was proud as his fist cut through the air. He was finally making his stand.

His pride dissipated in an instant, however, when the man caught his hand and jammed his cigar into the center of it's palm. Gabe howled in pain. The burn felt as if it was opening a hole in his hand. The agony was breathtaking. The suited man then slapped him in the mouth with an open hand and shoved him back into his seat.

"See what courage gets ya, kid? You're lucky I need you to be presentable for your visitors, or else I'd rip your buggy little eyes out and make you watch yourself being taught a stern lesson. Keep your fucking palm closed and that burn hidden. I don't care if it hurts. I'll carve it off with glass if these people get wind of it. Now sit there like a good little bitch and shut up." The man sat back down and puffed his cigar until it was evenly lit again. The smoke turned red as it rose to the ceiling. They sat in silence until the sound of footsteps appeared outside the room. They had a strange rhythm, as if the people they belonged to were skipping closer. The man rolled his eyes and swallowed what was left of the cigar.

The footsteps grew closer and closer until they stopped just outside of the room. The flat silver door pushed slowly open, flooding the room with the brightest light Gabe had ever seen. Rays blinded him and all he saw when he looked toward the door was white. The suited man didn't seem to be affected by it, or even to notice it. A second later the light expanded and engulfed Gabe, until he could see nothing but a white eternity.

Gabe woke in a panic, looking frantically around to get his bearings. He was confused by the absence of the light that enveloped him just moments before. Everything was dark now. It took him a few moments to realize that he had been dreaming. He was grateful to be awake and safe from the man in the suit, but slightly disappointed to not discover who had been coming for him. He rubbed his eyes and looked at his surroundings. The only light came from a weak table lamp. It took a little while for his eyes to adjust.

He was no longer in the street hiding behind a car and spying on the cop and his mother. Somehow, he had been brought to a room and placed on a couch. It was dark, and it took a little bit for his eyes to adjust. Once they did, he scanned the room. The walls were wood-paneled, with a lot of old photos framed and hung haphazardly. There was a desk in the corner with an old computer and papers scattered about it.

Gabe sat up on the couch, which was made of old leather and patched up in multiple places. The room smelled musty and reminded him of Allie's mother's apartment. He could hear muted activity outside of the room.

He pulled himself up off the couch and stood still for a moment to find his balance. He was still groggy from his sleep and was afraid to be too ambitious with his movement. There was a bottle of water on the table beside him. He guessed it was placed there for him by whoever brought him there. He was weary of the drink but needed refreshment desperately. He took it down in one gulp. Once he was confident in his ability to walk or run if needed, he crept toward the door to the room. He opened it a crack and peeked out. A nearly empty bar was on the other side. He could see a couple people sitting around at the far end of the building, with a couple rows of pool tables between them and himself. He figured that the room he was in must be the office, though not a very professional one.

He didn't believe he was in any danger, but if he was going to try to call the Morrisons, he wanted to do it elsewhere. He didn't know who had brought him there or why, but he wasn't going to stick around to find out. He would leave quickly and quietly, then find another business nearby with a phone. He looked forward to bringing the day's journey to an end.

To his right he saw a fire exit sign that led out the back of the building. The pool tables between him and the bar would cover him well if he stayed low to the ground. Whoever put him in that room was most likely still in the vicinity.

Gabe closed the door lightly behind him, then crouched down and began crawling toward his escape. He passed two pool tables quickly and stopped at the sight of a small paper on the floor, no bigger than a business card. On it was scribbled a name and a phone number.

ADRIEN

913-1314

After realizing its uselessness, Gabe tossed it aside and kept moving past a room labeled "The Rain Room." He was curious about what was in there, quite sure it wasn't rain. Muffled voices came from behind the door. Background made it impossible to make out the words. He kept moving without giving it another thought. The exit was down a very short hallway. Gabe hurried down it. He was afraid that opening the door would let in light and attract attention. He remembered the sun going down when he was last outside. It had to be dark now. He decided there wouldn't be any light streaming in.

1 ..., he thought. *2 ...*

Bang!

What sounded very much like a gunshot rang out behind him. The second it sounded, he pushed the door open and ran. He exited into an alley and arbitrarily turned left. He made it a dozen or so yards before he heard the door behind him being bashed open before it fully closed. He slid left behind a stack of wooden palettes and held his breath. Instinct told him that if this person found him, there would be plenty of trouble. Footsteps started in Gabe's direction, but before they got close, the door was once again opened with force before getting the chance to shut.

"Hey you, Doyle! Stop!" It was a man's voice, which happened to sound slightly familiar to Gabe. He tried to get a glimpse of the two strangers through the palettes, managing a decent view. They were too far away for him to clearly see facial details. The first man, whose back was to Gabe, raised a large, silver gun to his stalker. It took only a second to recognize the bright orange shirt with the black motorcycle silhouette. This was the cop who pulled over his mother. Gabe wondered where she was at that moment.

After a deep, winded breath, the second man continued, "What the fuck, man? Is that girl dead? Did you kill a girl in my fucking bar?" This man wore a flannel buttoned shirt and jeans. He looked tired, not just from the chase, but from life. Allie's brother Hugh had the same look. It was in the eyes. Allie told him it was because Hugh's life was filled to the brim with work.

He listened and expected the door to close behind the men, but the sound never came.

"Go back in the bar, Phil," the cop gasped. Gabe wasn't sure this guy was even a real police officer. He sure didn't act like one.

His back was to Gabe's hiding spot, but his voice indicated that he was also winded. "When the cops get here, tell them nothing about catching up to me. Tell them I was gone when you reached the alley. I swear to God if I find out you gave them any description of me, I'll send a fucking army to destroy everyone you care about."

Gabe's attention was drawn to the corner of the building, which partly hid a dark-skinned woman. He felt like he had seen her before, but the distance and darkness made him unsure. The whole scene was so absurd that he had to wonder if he was sleeping right now and merely entertaining himself with this dream.

The woman suddenly and quietly made an advance toward the men. Her swiftness was assassin-like. She grabbed the man named Phil and pressed something to his neck. Gabe could see the red handle of the object showing through her fingers. It looked just like his Swiss army knife.

"You've hurt a good deal of people without ever laying a hand upon them," the woman said from behind Phil, her mouth beside his ear. She had a deranged look of accomplishment on her face. "You've done so for a profit and without remorse or thought for the affect on their lives." Phil's eyes were wide open with a mix of terror and puzzlement. Gabe was horrified at the thought of what could happen next. "The police will never bring you to justice. God will send you to Hell when you die and I'm here to make sure that punishment is handed out immediately."

"No, please! I have a—" he started to beg.

The woman yanked her hand away, leaving a red line across Phil's neck. That line turned into a cascade of blood and he fell hard to the pavement. As he writhed on the ground, bleeding out, the two others stood in silence, watching him. The calmness and non-reaction of the cop was surreal. Gabe couldn't see his face to read his emotions but he could clearly see the woman absolutely flushed with satisfaction and joy. That was even more surreal. The sight of the blood made him dizzy. He struggled to hold himself back from vomiting.

The murderous woman's focus turned to the man who a short time ago was beating Gabe's mother.

"And who the fuck are you?" she said. He remained silent, his gun directed at her. "You never answered Phil's question about the girl. Is she dead? Did you kill her? You did, didn't you? She was lower than a cockroach and I won't mourn her for a second, but it's not your place to dispense justice." Was she talking about Gabe's mother? He felt a stab of panic and feared for her, despite his earlier resentment. He wanted to know she was safe.

The woman walked toward the man until a flash and a loud bang put a large, red dot in the center of her chest. Her face mutated from deranged and hateful to innocent and despairing.

"Please help me," she pleaded desperately, sounding like a different person altogether. She couldn't have been in her right mind, because she continued toward him without ever dropping the pocket knife. Gabe knew what that would bring, and he was correct. There were two more bangs and she dropped with a thud.

Gabe's weak stomach finally caught up to him and he threw up beside the palettes. Only a small amount came out, but the gagging was enough to give away his position. He returned his gaze to the cop, who met his eyes through the cover of the stack. Gabe sprinted instantly in the opposite direction of the bloodbath. His legs moved faster than they had ever been forced to before.

He heard two gunshots and expected to feel a hit, but none came. The end of the alley was near, where he would be able to take a hard turn and be out of the gun's line of fire. His safe haven drew closer and he heard another shot that didn't land. A second later, a force pushed his head harshly and he fell forward into darkness.

Gabe lay in the darkness in pieces. His limbs were scattered about the stone-walled room, but his head was still attached to his torso. There was no blood or gore to be found; instead the severed ends of his body resembled ripped cloth. He was a rag doll. And he was alone, save for the fly buzzing around near the ceiling.

He felt empty and lonely, and didn't want to be alive anymore. He didn't know if a rag doll could be killed, but he certainly hoped so. No one would miss him. There had never been a single soul who had cared about him. He knew nothing but apathy and cruelty in his short life. The thought of this made him cry. He wept for days, then weeks, then months.

It was impossible to tell how long he stayed trapped in this state before the door to the room swung open and two figures in white cloaks walked through. Their faces were hidden by hoods and he didn't know whether to welcome or fear them. Their bright, pristine garb shone brilliantly in contrast to the dingy gray and brown setting he was in. Without a word, the mysterious visitors gathered Gabe's limbs from around the room, taking great care not to damage them further. When they had all the pieces, they approached him and set them gently on the floor. They began moving the limbs around and lining them up with the places they had been severed from.

Sewing needles and yarn were pulled from their robes and each focused on a different limb, putting Gabe back together. They worked slowly and methodically, never speaking to each other or taking their gaze from their work. Their calm craft gave Gabe hope. Without a word they had convinced him that they could heal the wounds he accumulated over his few, harsh years.

It's going to be OK.

As they worked, the uninviting room began to brighten until the dark colors turned to white. The stone walls smoothed and became what looked like cotton. The transformation started on the ceiling and spread gradually down the walls.

When the figures each finished their first limb, they moved on to the next. Before long, Gabe could feel his fingers and toes again. He smiled in delight, and worked up the strength to wipe his tears with his newly regained hands. By now the entire room resembled a white cloud, and a great warmth washed over him.

The cloaked visitors stood up and helped him do the same. He faced them, unable to speak, but hoping his smile expressed how grateful he was. Simultaneously, the two raised their hands to their hoods and pulled them down. They were a man and a woman. Both radiated kindness. Gabe started crying again at the sight of their faces, not out of fear or emptiness, but from the greatest relief he had ever known.

The woman spoke softly, "Hello Gabe, it's nice to finally meet you. I'm Allie. This is Jack. We're going to take good care of you."

They both put a hand on one of his shoulders, then the man named Jack smiled.

"You're going to be alright, son. You're going to be alright."

Amy and Adrien's Schism

Adrien walked up to the door of Husky Harry's and stopped.

"I'm going to give you control again," he said to Amy. "Don't do anything stupid if you can manage such a responsibility, for fuck's sake. Just go in there and grab a drink. I'll be here watching for Phil and an opportunity to give him what he deserves. And don't fuck this up for me or I swear you're gonna find yourself with a steak knife in your gut."

Amy was once again in control of her body. "There's no need to threaten me, you evil prick. I already told you I'd gladly watch you put that slimy motherfucker down. Just don't do that shit in the open. I don't feel like running." A homeless man a couple dozen yards away was looking at Amy conversing with Adrien, trying to figure out if she was crazy. Amy and Adrien both noticed him, but neither cared about his puzzled stare. "And afterwards, we gotta get the fuck out of here, no more bullshitting. You're gonna fuck around and let Ron catch up to us."

Adrien didn't care at all about Ron; his mind was on Husky Harry's owner.

"Bitch, he isn't looking anywhere around these parts. We have all the time in the world. We can leave after I do this, and not a minute before. You fucking hear me? You better believe I could stay at the wheel here until I'm ready. I'm letting you drive out of the kindness of my fucking heart. Just fucking play some darts or something and don't try anything slick."

"Kindness my ass," Amy said without the will to keep up the back-and-forth. "Fine, I'm going."

She walked in and headed straight for the bar. If she was going to kill time, she wanted to do it with a Bloody Mary in her hand. There were only four men at the bar, none of them talking, just watching a soccer game on television. A blonde woman played pool by herself and a couple at a table were talking quietly. There was no sign of the owner as far as she could tell, though she didn't really know what to look for.

"Bloody Mary and a water, hun," Amy said to the bartender. "Please and thank you." He was a muscular twenty-something with brown, parted hair down to his shoulders. His name tag called him Jorge. She would have been trying to hook up plans for later if her present situation wasn't so fucked up.

"Sure thing," he responded with a smile.

She perused the place with her eyes and saw the disgusting room in the back with a sign above it that read, "The Rain Room." After tonight, no more women were going to be hurt within those walls.

A minute later she had a drink in each hand and was walking toward the pool tables. She thought she might as well spend this spare time showing the lonely blonde how to play some pool. The woman had just finished clearing the table and was about to rack another set. She was thin and gorgeous, but dressed plainly. She wore jeans and a baby blue sweater with the sleeves rolled up to her elbows.

"You interested in some competition?" Amy asked.

"Only if you're actually worthy of being called competition," the woman teased without hesitation. She had a perfect confidence. Amy liked her already.

"I'd like to think I qualify. Name's Amy."

"I'm Sandra. I only play 9-Ball. Newcomer racks."

Amy grabbed the rack and Sandra started retrieving the balls from the pockets and rolling them toward her. Amy racked them nice and tight, and Sandra broke, getting the 1 and 7 balls in.

"So what do you do to get by?" Sandra asked as she aimed for the 2 ball.

"I'm a dog groomer," Amy lied. She suspected the game would end abruptly if she answered the question with, "I sleep with men for money."

"You're awfully devoid of bites and scratches for someone who clips Chihuahuas all day." She sunk the 2 ball.

"I'm a *skilled* groomer. And I'm a dog whisperer. That helps me convince them not to maul me. Not the Chihuahuas, though; those little guys only speak Spanish and they can't understand me." Amy was shamelessly flirting at this point. It was just for fun, she had no interest in women who weren't paying her. "What about you?"

"I'm a UFO investigator," Sandra joked as she struck the cue ball, getting the 3 in the corner pocket. "Or a pharmacist, whichever you find more interesting."

"Let's go with UFO investigator," Amy said with a giggle. "Tell me … you believe in all that stuff?"

"UFOs? No. Aliens? Yes."

"Really? You don't strike me as the type."

"Ha, 'the type,'" Sandra said, amused. Her phone chimed three times in her pocket. She pulled it out and checked what the chimes brought in. She appeared to be texting as she continued to speak. "My *type* is logical and logic says that aliens are out there. Our sun is one star out of hundreds of billions in our galaxy. Our galaxy is one out of hundreds of billions in the universe. To say that our star is the only one with intelligent life spinning around it would be quite the leap of faith. People think I'm crazy, but I've always said I wanna be abducted by aliens." She leaned over the table taking aim at the 4.

"You *are* crazy!" Amy gasped as Sandra got the 4 ball in the side. "What if all the anal probe nonsense turned out to be true?"

"Then I'd be in pain and walking funny. But seriously, hear me out on this one. The question of other intelligent beings is one of life's biggest mysteries. Probably *the* biggest besides the after-life." She stopped playing now, clearly enthusiastic about the topic. "To come in contact with alien life would be worth enduring anything they could put me through. Not many people, if any, would get that chance. I feel the same way about ghost and demons. I wish I'd get haunted so I could know for sure if there is life after death."

Amy didn't know how to react to the last part without either sounding crazy or pissing off Adrien.

"I don't think knowing about aliens would be worth an anal probe. And I don't think I'd want a demon around either. I read a book about a girl who was possessed by a demon who used her to kill bad people. It seemed like a miserable existence."

"A vigilante demon, huh? Now that sounds like an interesting read." Sandra tried for the 5 ball and missed, getting a scratch in the process.

"Kinda sucked, actually." Amy wondered whether Adrien was listening in to this bit. She grabbed the cue ball from the pocket and lined it up with the 5 and a corner pocket. She tapped the cue ball lightly on the bottom so it rolled backwards after hitting the 5, giving her a perfect shot on the 6. "I'm more of a *Goosebumps* type of reader. Y'know, 4th grade level reading."

"I loved *Goosebumps*!" Sandra shrieked. "I swear you'd get your arm gnawed off if you tried to tear me away from that shit when I was a kid."

Amy hit the 6 ball in, then missed the 8. "Only thing I ever read now is *Cosmo*."

"Ugh!" Sandra said, making a disgusted face. She went on to mockingly quote their headlines. "'How to Tell if You're Man is Really Into You,' '5 Things That Will Drive Your Man Crazy,' 'Does He Really Like it When You Shave?'" They both chuckled. "There's only one thing you need to do to keep a man happy, Amy – and don't let anyone tell you differently. Here's the big secret: just touch him. Men are stupid, simple creatures with stupid, simple needs." She hit the 8 ball in with ease.

"I think you got it all figured out. Now hurry up and miss the 9 so I can finish this game," Amy said teasingly.

Sandra didn't miss it. They played four more games after that, Amy losing all except one of them. Their conversation led them through religion, crazy boyfriend stories, Sandra's college memories, family vacations, the worst movies of all time, the best movies of all time, comic books, social media, what to avoid when in Aruba and tips on improving Amy's pool playing. There wasn't a single moment of awkward silence between them. The two exchanged information before Sandra had to leave to meet someone.

Amy put the card marked with Sandra's number into her pocket and made her way back to the bar to order another Bloody Mary. She had barely taken one sip of it when she heard a man – who had appeared next to her suddenly – address Jorge.

"Excuse me sir, could you point me in the direction of the owner please?" Amy turned around and saw a short, husky man accompanied by a woman. He had on an extremely bright orange t-shirt, the chest of which was covered by his gray beard. He looked like a creep. No doubt he had skeletons in his closet that would make him a candidate for Adrien's justice. The woman with him was beautiful but disheveled. She was looking at the ground, causing her long, blonde hair to cover most of her face.

"He got here just a minute ago," Jorge responded. "He's in the back office. I'll grab him for you."

"Good man," the bearded guy said. He and the blonde both sat at the bar a couple stools away. When the girl finally looked up, Amy was taken aback by a terrible scar that stretched across her forehead. She thought it was a damn shame to have a face like that sullied by such an unfortunate mark. The girl was melancholy. She looked tired, as if she had no desire to be there, especially with this man.

"Can I get you two something while you wait?" Jorge asked them.

"I'll take a CC and Seven. What do you want, Faith?"

"I'm good," she said in a low voice.

"Get her a water," the man said the bartender.

"Sure thing."

They hadn't even gotten their drinks when Phil emerged from the office, which was at the back of the bar, past the pool tables. Its door was next to the Rain Room's.

"There he is now, sir," Jorge said and motioned to him.

"Stay here," the man told Faith sternly. "Don't think about leaving. I'll take you down to the station or worse if you try anything dumb." He got up and walked over to Phil, who was taken by surprise when he was approached by the burly man.

As soon as he was a good distance away, Amy moved over so that she was beside the blonde. "Name's Amy, hun. What's yours?" She spoke as warmly as she could manage.

"Huh?" the woman said, startled to suddenly see someone so close to her. "Oh … uh, Faith. My name's Faith." Amy was positive she had heard that name recently, but couldn't think of where.

"Lovely name. Now Faith, I couldn't help but notice you seem to be in an awfully unpleasant situation with your man-friend over there."

"He's not my friend – and keep out of my business," Faith said defensively. She was understandably annoyed at a complete stranger giving their two cents about her circumstance.

"I only mention it because if that's a bad man you got yourself tangled up with, I can help you out. I happen to know someone who doesn't take kindly to men who treat women badly."

After over an hour of silence, Adrien made himself heard, clearly not happy with Amy for volunteering his services to this pathetic stranger.

"Fuck that, you cretinous shrew, I'm not helping anyone," he said in his deepest, harshest tone to Amy. It made her slightly nervous.

Faith was both terrified and confused at this outbreak. "I, uh …" she started, but had no clue how to react.

"Not that I'd help such a piss-poor example of a woman

anyhow," Adrien persisted. "She's a worm who will do anything for a fix. Just look at her arms." Adrien spoke this to Amy as if Faith wasn't even present. She just sat there dumbfounded.

Adrien then turned his abuse directly to her. "Scum. I bet you'd sell your own kid to get high for five minutes. People like you contribute nothing to this world and bring the rest of humanity down. You just take and take, then wallow in your own pettiness, wearing it like a fucking badge."

"You have no fucking clue who I am or how I live," Faith said, desperate to defend herself. Adrien knew his words were hitting her hard and was amused by her inability to counter his assessments. The few customers who were still in the bar were taking notice of their exchange, but their voices were too low to carry clearly throughout the place. Phil and the Faith's partner were unaware of any of it, and Jorge wasn't around to intervene.

"I know exactly how you live," Adrien countered. "Like a fucking rat! I bet that scar you carry is drug-related. Just another souvenir of your lifestyle, along with your track marks. Your entire being reeks of trash."

"You're fucking crazy, you psycho bitch," Faith said, nearly crying. "And you don't look like a fucking prize yourself. Talking like you're contributing shit to this world. Look at you, with your ragged clothes and ratty hair. You look like a damn hook—" she was cut off by the man in orange. Amy and Adrien both knew the end of her sentence.

"What's all the fuss about, Faith?" he asked, acting like a hero there to save the day. "And who the fuck is this?"

"It's no one." Faith got off the stool and stood face-to-face with the man. "Are we doing this or what?" she asked impatiently.

"Right this way, firecracker." He motioned toward the back

of the bar to the Rain Room. Adrien and Amy knew what she was in for. Faith stormed away toward the room; the man followed shaking his head.

You are just completely incapable of being low-key, you know that? Amy thought to Adrien.

He kept control of her, watching Phil intently. He'd taken over duties at the bar so that Jorge could take a break. He approached them.

"Need a refill?" Amy was surprised by how likable he seemed.

Adrien refused another drink and followed Phil with her eyes as he went to work cleaning the cabinets behind the bar. Amy could physically feel Adrien's hatred for the man and was surprised at the discipline he exhibited by keeping his cool in close proximity to him.

"Excuse me," a young man's voice said from behind them. There was urgency in the tone. Adrien turned, expressionless, his mind consumed in his mission. Amy noticed the man's slight uneasiness in her appearance. She could only imagine how she looked after the day she'd had. There wasn't much time to worry about appearance when being used as a murderous puppet. Adrien just stared at him, waiting for him to continue.

"Have you seen a blonde girl come through here? Late twenties with a long scar across her forehead." He had a hopeful look in his eyes.

"Haven't seen her," Adrien said flatly and turned back to the Bloody Mary.

What? Amy thought to him. *That girl clearly needed help and was probably waiting for this fella to come along. Fuck this, I'm telling him.*

"*I* saw her." Amy exclaimed and turned back around toward the man, perhaps too enthusiastically. Never before had she been able to forcefully regain control from Adrien. It was liberating for her, though she didn't know if he had let her do it. It sure felt like she had beaten him, but who knew? "She went in the Rain Room with some man, just minutes ago. There it is, over there." Amy directed his gaze toward the back of the bar to the door. "But I bet it's locked."

"Thanks a—" the man began but was abruptly stopped by the sound of a gunshot. The two of them winced and ducked a bit, then frantically looked around for the origin. Just then, the door to the Rain Room flung open. The man who arrived with Faith burst out of it. He made a beeline for the back door of the bar. Phil burst from behind the counter and ran full speed after him.

Adrien knew his opportunity had arrived. He effortlessly snatched Amy's body back from her and headed after Phil, accidentally knocking Faith's rescuer to the floor. The chaos of the scene was everything Adrien could have hoped for, short of catching Phil alone and secluded.

He reached the back exit and caught the door before it shut from the two men going through it. He didn't know if they were right outside or if the chase had led them away from the bar. As he opened the door wider, he heard the men but couldn't see them. They were around the corner in the alley.

"Is that girl dead? Did you kill a girl in my fucking bar?" Phil's voice asked, fighting for breath. Adrien closed the door quietly behind him.

"Go back in the bar, Phil," the other man said, equally out of breath. "When the cops get here, tell them nothing about catching up to me. Tell them I was gone when you reached the alley. I swear to God if I find out you gave them any description of me, I'll send a fucking army to destroy everyone you care about." Adrien peeked around the corner to find Phil's back to him. The shooter held a pistol that was aimed at Phil's face.

Adrien was salivating with excitement. This was it. He pulled Amy's Swiss army knife from her pocket and ran up behind Phil, grabbing him and pressing the blade to his throat. Amy was astonished by how fast it all happened. Both Phil and the bearded man were stupefied by the seemingly random appearance of this third party.

Adrien spoke into Phil's ear. "You've hurt a good deal of people without ever laying a hand upon them. You've done so for a profit and without remorse or thought for the affect on their lives." The man with the gun kept it leveled and aimed toward Adrien and Phil. "The police will never bring you to justice. God will send you to Hell when you die and I'm here to make sure that punishment is handed out immediately."

Stop, Adrien! You can't do this! Amy screamed at him internally. The whole thing was wrong, her mind was changed. She didn't want to see this man die.

"No, please! I have a—" Phil started.

Adrien pulled the knife across his neck with all his force and dropped the gurgling waste of life to the ground. He and the shooter in orange both watched Phil die. There was a silence between them, a mutual satisfaction. Adrien stood in complete bliss, letting his deed wash over him like a long-awaited compensation for a job well done. The other man watched intently as Phil bled out.

Adrien turned his attention to him. "And who the fuck are you?" He gave the man a second to answer, but his shock hadn't worn off yet. "You never answered Phil's question about the girl. Is she dead? Did you kill her? You did, didn't you? She was lower than a cockroach and I won't mourn her for a second, but it's not your place to dispense justice."

Adrien took a step toward the bearded man – knife still in hand, covered in blood. Before he could take another step, the man pulled the trigger and put a round in the center of Amy's chest. Adrien barely gave it any thought, but inside, Amy was horrified. She was going to die here in an alley for something she had no part of. Something she witnessed as a helpless bystander. She hated Adrien for bringing her to this, and she wasn't about to die as a puppet on strings. She would at very least show Adrien that in their last moments, he was *not* in control. Command of her body was once again hers. She managed to stay on her feet.

"Please help me," she pleaded to the man who had shot her seconds earlier. If luck was on her side, he would realize that she was no longer the maniac who had just murdered a man in cold blood. She moved toward him, her common sense veiled by adrenaline and panic. He shot two more times and dropped her to the ground. She was still alive, but knew she would never get up again.

A few seconds later, Amy saw a small person, perhaps a child appear from behind a dark stack of something and run in the opposite direction toward the street. The man with the gun aimed it and shot twice, but the mysterious little person was still running. Amy had no clue who it was, but she hoped they would fare better than she had. Two more shots were enough to drop the runner. Her hope was gone. The gunner then made a break for it, leaving

Amy alone in the alley dying.

"Tell me something before I die, Adrien," she said, struggling to get the words out through bloody gurgles. "Why did you rub blood under the eyes of the people you killed?" She coughed violently. "And don't give me no aggressive shit-talking. Be straight with me, you owe me that much."

We did it, Adrien said, speaking to her through thought for the first time ever, *because those sinners lived empty lives. They died empty deaths. No sadder existence is imaginable. And so they'll weep for eternity with tears of blood.*

"*You* deserve to die and weep for eternity," she said. She meant Adrien, but as the words left her lips, she realized the same went for her.

We both do, Adrien whispered, his voice fading gradually in her head. *You, for wasting your life as a whore. Me, for the killing. He's going to send me right back to the fire. You shouldn't expect any different.*

"As long as you're nowhere near me when we arrive, I'll take it."

④
③

⑤

FIRE
EXIT

R...
⑥

②

TABLES

①

Phil's Tragedy

"With his foe defeated, the brave knight pulled the princess onto his massive dragon, and the three flew away from peril. The hero's great quest had ensured peace and happiness throughout the land, and all was well once again." Phil closed the book and set it on the night stand.

"I don't get it," said seven-year-old Jordan, who should have been tired by now but wasn't.

"And what don't you get?"

"Well," she said with her head tilted in confusion, "Sendax the dragon could breathe fire, right? They even said it was hot enough to melt stone! So why did the knight have to go into the castle to fight the Dark Necromancer? Couldn't Sendax just burn the whole place down, bad guy and all?" She looked at him with wide eyes, expecting a concise answer. Her inquisitiveness was her greatest charm.

Phil thought quickly. "Well … he was far too honorable a knight to destroy the Dark Necromancer without a fair fight!" He scanned her face for a gauge of his success. She nodded and seemed satisfied with his answer. He smiled at her. "I have to go to work now, Munchkin. Have Heather call me if you need anything. And I already told her your bedtime is 9:30, so don't try to fool her."

"Wouldn't dream of it Daddy," she joked, quoting a phrase she heard on television. She flashed a huge smile at him.

"Of course you wouldn't." He kissed her smooth, bald head and stood up. "Love and kisses, Munchkin."

"Love and kisses, Daddy," she said, then picked up the book to read herself.

Phil walked into the kitchen, where the babysitter was eating leftover pizza. "I'm out of here, Heather. Give me a ring if anything comes up. Her medication is on top of the fridge, she knows which ones she needs before bed."

"Roger that, big guy," she said in jest. Phil liked her. She was the only eighteen-year-old on the planet he would trust with Jordan. Her leukemia was getting worse by the week, and her mother left Phil with no reliable help. He owed Heather everything he had for being there to watch Jordan while he worked.

He headed out the door and got into his car. His commute to work – a bar called Husky Harry's – was a whopping four miles. His father built the business by hand, and for some reason felt the need to name it ridiculously. Phil became the owner when he died, and didn't have the heart to take his father's name down, foolish as it was. It wasn't the prettiest establishment, but Husky Harry's was the sole reason he could continue to support Jordan. That made it the most important thing in his life, after her. Business sucked recently, but if he gave up the finer things in life, it allowed him to keep her treatment going. When he was with Jordan's mother – who's name he never spoke – he had been living far more than comfortably. She was a stripper and he owned a bar, so together they lived the good life. Not that they didn't have their problems, chief among them was her being a cunt.

People were always shocked to hear him call her that, until he told them how she ran off when she learned that her daughter's illness meant tightening their spending. Then they understood. He heard from her only once in the year since Jordan's diagnosis, and it turned out she was looking for money. The woman disgusted him, most of all when he had to fend off Jordan's increasingly frequent questions about her.

He realized he was driving like a maniac just thinking about it and slowed down to the speed limit. The last thing he needed was a ticket and a higher insurance bill.

He was about a half mile from the bar when he spotted something curious on the side of the road. It appeared to him to be a kid lying behind a parked car. He pulled over a few yards past it, and reversed to get closer. Then he hopped out of the car and walked briskly over, confirming his suspicion. It was a young, blonde boy with a backpack laying motionless on the pavement.

Phil crouched and put a hand on the face-down boy's arm. "Wake up, buddy. *Psst.* Wake up." When no answer came, he felt a sense of dread and immediately checked the boy's pulse. He was alive, but completely unresponsive and breathing very lightly. Phil searched through his pockets, but didn't find anything in the way of identification. The backpack he was wearing produced nothing either. It contained mostly random objects. Some snacks, soda, a surprising amount of cash and some other, useless items. There was, however, an envelope containing a letter. It was addressed to a Mr. and Mrs. Morrison. The address would be no help to him. He was better off calling the police than hunting down strange houses.

Phil saw cell phones as an unnecessary expense, and had recently gotten rid of his. He was always either at home or in the bar, and money was tight. Calling the police or an ambulance wasn't possible right then. He had to take the kid to the bar and call from there. He turned the boy over carefully to make sure he wasn't injured. When Phil was satisfied, he lifted him up and carried him to his car. It was much like the way he carried Jordan into the house when she fell asleep during late car rides. Sometimes she even pretended to be sleeping just so he would. She thought she was clever, but he knew her scheme. Luckily for her, he was more than happy to be her taxi.

Phil placed the boy into the passenger seat and buckled him in. He took a look at the young face in the car's interior light and guessed that he was ten or so. His lips were moving, but no sound escaped.

Then, in a hushed tone, he said what Phil could only make out to be, "I saw the Pope with lollipops." He couldn't help but chuckle a bit at the preposterous murmur. He smiled and shut the passenger-side door. Not only had the random sentence amused him, but it also gave him the comforting impression that the kid was indeed only sleeping, though quite heavily.

He drove the remaining distance to the bar without a peep from his tranquil passenger. He parked in the lot located on the side of Husky Harry's and carried the boy in. Jorge the bartender was occupied with one of the very few customers, so he didn't notice Phil's arrival until he was at the office door. He shot Phil a confused glance, clearly puzzled by the bundle in his arms. Without letting go of the mystery child, Phil put up his index finger to communicate, "One minute." He struggled, but succeeded in getting the door open despite his burden, then placed the boy on the couch. He planned to grab the emergency phone list from behind the bar counter and search for the number to the police station. He figured that was the best way to settle this, since 9-1-1 would probably have been overkill for the situation. He didn't think he'd be gone more than a couple minutes, but in case the kid woke up, Phil left a bottle of water on the side table.

He left the room, closing the door quietly behind him, and strode past the pool tables toward the bar. Halfway to his destination, he was intercepted by a rough-looking bearded man in a bright orange shirt. He looked like a biker; Phil would have bet cash that the back of that shirt had a motorcycle on it. His beard was gray and impressive in size and thickness.

The man extended a hand. "Phil, right?"

"That's right, what can I do for ya?" Phil said, accepting the handshake.

"Name's Doyle. Wanted to talk to you about rentin' the Rain Room for 'bout an hour."

Ugh, Phil thought, hoping his face didn't give away his feelings. This was exactly the type of person he didn't want renting the room, though the very nature of it attracted them in droves.

The Rain Room was a gift and a curse. The idea for it was put into his head by a friend and would have been a complete blessing had it not turned out to be so sleazy. It was a room in the back of the building, next to the office that was set up to be a sort of lounge. Customers could rent it by the hour and were given complete privacy, but could still order drinks and have them delivered if they wished. The room brought seriously needed revenue, but that positive was just about offset by the trouble it caused.

A few months ago, a girl had been drugged and raped in the room. Phil was devastated. *Still* was, to the point where he wanted to shut it down. The only reason he didn't discontinue renting it out was that he had come to rely on the income for Jordan's treatments. He may have been able to get by without it, but their living situation would have suffered greatly. *Women get raped in hotels too*, he reasoned, *and the owners aren't left with muddy consciences.* Unfortunately, this logic did little to alleviate his feeling of guilt.

The situation got far worse when the girl got it into her head that *he* had supplied the rapist with the drugs and helped cover it up afterwards. It was the sickest thing Phil ever heard, and the accusation scorched him inside. Thankfully the police found no evidence whatsoever to support it, and after an hour of questioning he was let go. Following the incident, he refused to rent the room past eleven o'clock and sometimes downright turned certain people away. He couldn't terminate it entirely though. He needed it. He was leery about letting this Doyle use it, but he was basing that on appearance alone, and that didn't sit well with him.

"Sure, I'll just need an ID and credit card to hold on to. It's just for security, you can pay however."

"Uh … OK. No problemo, captain," the man said with a hoarse voice. He reached into his back pocket and fumbled through his wallet for his card, then handed it to Phil. The card identified the man as Casey O'Doyle.

"So your last name's O'Doyle and that turned into your nickname being Doyle?" Phil asked suspiciously.

"Yup. Just don't go calling me Doyle O'Doyle, please and thank you," he threw back casually.

"Alright then. You can order any food and drinks you want using the phone in the room to call Jorge at the bar. Any tab you rack up can be paid off before you leave, along with the cost of the room, which is sixty an hour."

"A dollar a minute, my OCD likes that very much," the man

said, smiling with yellow teeth. The smirk reeked of insincerity. "Thanks a lot Phil, have yourself a fine night."

"You too, pal," Phil said and walked toward the bar. Doyle did the same, splitting to retrieve his girlfriend, who was talking with a nutty-looking black woman. The Orange District brought in all types. After a few seconds, the couple walked off towards the Rain Room.

"Well that's a rather sketchy fella, huh?" Jorge said to Phil with a smirk.

"How often do non-sketchy guys rent out the Rain Room?" he countered with a chuckle. He poured himself a glass of water, then grabbed the emergency contact list and dialed the police. He explained his discovery to the operator and was informed that an officer should be there in about fifteen minutes. *Good thing it's not an emergency*, he thought, but kept his criticism to himself.

He took over the bar and let Jorge take a break. There weren't many patrons in the place, so he took the time to clean out some of the cabinets under the bar.

He was moving on to the second cabinet when he heard a furious noise that could only have been a gunshot. He jumped up and looked immediately to the office door. He was relieved to see it still closed. Before the relief could truly sink in, the door to the Rain Room opened and the bearded man dashed out toward the fire exit. Without thinking, Phil sprang from behind the bar and pursued him. He zig-zagged between pool tables effortlessly and pushed the exit door open with authority. He emerged into the alley just in time to see Doyle turn the corner.

He followed and yelled, "Hey you, Doyle! Stop!" The man responded by swinging around and pointing a menacing silver pistol in Phil's face. He was terrified, but he could see that the other man was equally so. His countenance displayed pure guilt and desperation. Phil feared the worst. He was fighting to catch his breath, but managed to get out, "What the fuck, man? Is that girl dead? Did you kill a girl in my fucking bar?"

"Go back in the bar, Phil," Doyle demanded, also panting. It had struck Phil as strange when the man addressed him by name earlier, but now it was surreal. This mysterious figure was speaking to him as if he knew him, which made the loaded weapon all the more unsettling. He continued, "When the cops get here, tell them nothing about catching up to me. Tell them I was gone when you reached the alley. I swear to God if I find out you gave them any description of me, I'll send a fucking army to destroy everyone you care about." Phil got the point. He knew he couldn't risk anything stupid that could leave Jordan parentless. He didn't even know why he had followed the man, it wasn't his battle.

He was about to turn and retreat when he was grabbed from behind. He saw shock in Doyle's eyes and simultaneously felt the cold metal of what he assumed was a blade touch his neck. He went limp so as to not tempt this perplexing assailant, then heard a harsh voice speak into his ear.

"You've hurt a good deal of people without ever laying a hand upon them. You've done so for a profit and without remorse or thought for the affect on their lives." The speaker was a female, but the evil and animosity that spewed from her mouth belonged to a deranged male. Confusion swept over Phil. He was a good, honest man by all accounts that mattered. He lived a humble life. He couldn't understand why this stranger would want to hurt him, or what she meant when she said he hurt others. Phil's life was in the hands of a completely unstable and mistaken individual, and he had already been in one of the strangest and most frightening moments of his life before this development. Were the two connected? Was this a twisted coincidence?

"The police will never bring you to justice," the confused psychopath continued. "God will send you to Hell when you die and I'm here to make sure that punishment is handed out immediately." Phil had never known terror like he had in that moment. Not the time he was thrown from a moving vehicle, nor the time he was mugged at gunpoint. Even the moment Jordan was diagnosed with leukemia paled in comparison to this. At least then he had known that in sickness or in health, he could make sure her life was worth living. The danger he was in now threatened to leave her with nothing. She was too frail to survive an existence like that. His death would mean hers as well. All this flashed through his mind in an instant. He had been an atheist for as long as he could remember, but he hoped now that he was wrong.

"No, please! I have a—" *daughter who needs me.*

Before he could finish his plea, there was a sudden movement and he felt a sharp sensation of coldness in his throat, then a stream of warmth. She really did it. He couldn't believe it was going to end this way. His body ceased to work and he fell. As he lay there knowing he would die, he didn't feel pain. He wasn't afraid of death. He wasn't concerned with why this had happened. He was troubled only by the thought of the most precious child the world had ever known being left alone. It was a cold and unust fate. There was solace for him, though, in the thought of their last words to each other.

Love and kisses, Munchkin.
Love and kisses, Daddy.

Faith's End

"License and registration," the cop said, eyeing Faith through a pair of sunglasses. Faith had to assume he was a cop, since he wasn't wearing a uniform. Instead he wore an orange t-shirt and jeans. He had a full, gray beard and looked like he would fit in more with a biker gang than a police force. He *was* driving a cruiser, but in this city that could easily mean it was stolen and the man at her window was a psychopath.

She had a bit of a dilemma. She wanted proof that this man was an officer, but in the case that he was, she didn't want to aggravate him by asking for it. Any unnecessary inquisition was a gamble, seeing as how she had an absurd amount of heroin and a pistol underneath a sweatshirt beside her. She chose to ask for proof.

"Sorry Officer, but could I please see some ID?" She talked mechanically, just as she did whenever she was in the presence of cops. He seemed understanding and produced his badge from his pocket without a word. She had hoped it would be a photo ID. A badge proved nothing. "Um, sir … I don't mean to be a pain, but is there any chance you have a photo ID?"

"You're an awfully untrustin' little lady," the officer said, annoyed. He reached into his back pocket and pulled out his wallet.

"Sorry sir, but it's a messed up world out there."

He showed her the police ID. "Indeed it is. Now, license and registration please." She was ready with both in her hand before the officer had even reached her truck. She handed them to him through the window.

He looked at the license. "Tell me somethin' ... Faith. Where'd that blood on your right hand come from?"

Her eyes shot to her hand on the steering wheel, which sure enough had blood on the top of it.

How did I not notice?

"I, um ..." In her panic she couldn't think of a single excuse. She stammered for a few seconds, but nothing close to a sentence was formed.

"Why don't you go ahead and step out of the vehicle darlin'. And leave the pocketbook in there." He opened her door for her. This was just her luck. She cursed herself for taking the drugs and gun from Paul. There was no reason of merit for her to have held on to them even this long.

She climbed out – defeated and scared shitless – and was directed to stand at the back of the truck with her hands on the tailgate. She was going to jail, she just knew it. There was no chance the cop would leave the truck unsearched, and she hadn't even really hidden the stash. A strong wind could come along and reveal her secret. She struggled to hold back tears as she stood in anticipation.

"I'm gonna take a look through the vehicle, you just stay right here." He walked toward the passenger-side door. Every step he took drained hope from her. He opened the door and immediately fixated on the sweatshirt that covered her guilt. She could see him rummaging under it through the cab's rear window.

"Whoa!" he shouted from inside. He exited the truck with Paul's gun in his hand and walked toward her. "Why don't you go ahead and tell me what a little lady like yourself is doing with this." His tone frightened her. It suggested that she wasn't just in trouble with the law, but with him personally.

"I found it up the street," she lied, knowing it would fail to convince. "I was on my way to turn it in just now."

"Right, right. Of course," he said sarcastically. He hunched over so that he was only a few inches from her face. "And I'm guessin' you just stumbled upon a boatload of dope too, didn't you? You're a lyin' little jezebel. Do I have 'dumbass' written on my fuckin' forehead darlin'? Well I suppose I must. Why the fuck else would a dumb little bitch like yourself tell me some stupid shit like that?" This wasn't how a cop should act, and she sure as hell wasn't going to sit by and take the abuse. She had just shot a known killer in the arm and ran away with his gun and dope. Telling off this donut-eating motherfucker would be child's play. The worst he could do was put her in a cell, which she was sure to end up in anyhow.

"You can believe whatever the fuck you wanna believe," she said venomously. She expected him to cuff her. Or scold her. Or yell at her. She didn't expect him to hit her. He *did*, and the blow sent pain from its landing spot on her chin to every corner of her body. She dropped to her knees, seeing spots. It had come so fast that the surprise was just as paralyzing as the pain. "You have no right, you ugly son-of-a—" he hit her again before she could finish the sentence. This one struck her cheek and sent her to the ground, face-down. She feared for her life for the second time in a half hour.

"I have the right to do whatever the fuck I please, buttercup. Y'know why? 'Cause I'm a motherfuckin' officer of the law, and you're just a tramp who wouldn't be missed if I fucked you right here and left you dead in the street.

"Get up," he said, walking back to his cruiser. "Get in the back of the car. And don't try to fight it, 'cause if you play your cards right, I ain't even gonna bring you in to the station."

Faith already had pain and fear to contend with; that last sentence added confusion. She made it back up to her knees after some struggling. "If ... if we're not going to the station, why do I need to get into the back of the car?"

He turned around and looked at her. "You need to get in the car 'cause otherwise you're lookin' at a whole lotta time in the pen with all them goodies you got." He opened the cruiser's rear door. "We're gonna take a ride, have a talk, and maybe if you're well behaved, I'll send you on your way. Without the goodies, of course."

A short time later, and after a more thorough search of Faith's truck, the squad car pulled away.

"Where are you taking me?" Faith asked from the backseat. She put on her sweatshirt, which the cop brought from her truck.

"What I want from you, Faith, is to tell me the truth about how you obtained a pistol and that obscene amount of dope," he said, ignoring her question and gesturing toward the trunk, where he had stored her spoils. "Off the record, I promise. I already told you, if you do as I say and don't ask questions, you'll be back to your car in a couple hours."

"I shot a drug dealer and stole his shit," she said, knowing perfectly well it would come off like a joke.

"Mm-hmm. Keep sassin' me girl and you'll see what it gets ya."

"What?" she asked defiantly. "Another punch to the face? I didn't do anything to deserve this."

"You're right. Perfectly innocent. I've seen thousands of innocent ladies ridin' 'round with massive amounts of drugs and a gun. Yup, classic misunderstanding." He cleared his throat. "Let's cut the crap. I know I probably didn't make the best impression back there, but I had to establish my dominance. I hope you understand now what kind of man you're dealin' with.

"See, to me you're just a junkie, plain and simple. I could bring you in and put you through the system, I could kill you, or I could let you go free. Luckily for you, I'm goin' with the latter. Of course freedom ain't never free. I need something from you, which I'll explain in just a minute. Now, I want you to keep those three options of mine in your head for the next hour or so, because I'm not committed to letting you go. If it's more trouble than it's worth, I have no problem with either of the other two possibilities, though the second would be the more attractive one. No paperwork."

He pulled to the side of the road and shut the car off. His gaze remained forward. "About a quarter mile in that direction," he said, pointing ahead, "is a bar called Husky Harry's."

"Yeah, I've driven by it plenty of times," she said uninterested. She couldn't believe this asshole was talking to her as if he didn't just punch her in the fucking face. Twice.

"Three months ago," he continued, "a girl was drugged and raped there. And she's not the only one that it's happened to. Ya see, the owner has this dirty little room he calls the 'Rain Room.'

What he does is rents this room out by the hour like a motel. Now, right off the bat you can see why that would be a horrible idea. You got drunk guys bringin' drunk girls in there, and anything can happen. It gets worse. The owner has a scheme going on, where he'll actually sell roofies to men rentin' the room out. Sick, right?

"I know at this point you probably don't think of me as a man with a strong set of morals. Hell, I won't pretend I am. That girl I mentioned though – the one that got raped – that's my niece. She came right to me after it happened, crying like a terrified child. Broke my fuckin' heart. We brought the owner in and charged him with aidin' and abettin' a rape. I wanted that damn place shut down for good and to put that grimy fuck behind bars. But there wasn't enough evidence, ya see? So he went free. As a man who believes in true justice, I can't continue to let that happen."

"So … you see rape as wrong, but beating and *threatening* to rape a woman you pull over is OK with you?"

"First off, you're hardly a woman. You're a piece of dirt with dangerous and illegal items on ya, whose life is already down the shitter from stickin' yourself with a spike. Yeah, I saw the marks. Secondly, it's for the greater good. A couple punches and a threat to a junkie is surely justified when you think of how many girls are gonna be helped."

"How does hitting me help anyone?" Faith was starting to feel like a pawn in a game she didn't know about.

"Ah, I'm gettin' to that part. See, I've been waitin' outside Paul Wilcox's house for a little bit for a strung out bitch like you to go waltzin' in and buy some drugs. His filthy business is pretty well-known around these parts, especially to police, and it was only a matter of time before I caught somethin' on my hook that I could use. That's where you came in and drew the short straw. I was only expectin' my fishy to have a small bag on them, but you gave me quite the ammo for blackmail, no pun intended. So I find your stash, beat you up a little, bare my teeth. Like I said, show you I'm not fuckin' around. And that brings us here.

"I'm gonna take you into that bar and rent an hour in the Rain Room. After a little bit, I'm gonna leave and you're gonna stay behind. Then you're gonna call the police and tell them you were raped in there and you saw that dirtbag owner give me a pill beforehand. There's no way he's gonna survive a second accusation. Even if he never sees a conviction, Husky Harry's reputation will be ruined.

"So the decision you have, Miss Faith, is this: are you gonna tell a little lie that will ensure the safety of God knows how many girls, or are you gonna refuse and leave me with the tougher decision of what to do with you?"

"Guess I don't have much of a choice, do I?" Faith asked rhetorically with her arms crossed.

"There's always a choice," he said, turning and looking at her in the backseat for the first time. "Sometimes the options just suck a whole lot."

"You can dress it up, but I still don't have a real choice. So … what are we waiting for?"

"The owner, that's what. Name's Phil, he lives a couple miles back. Should be headin' into work any minute now and he'll pass right by us. I need him to be in the joint when this goes down."

"You sure did your homework on this one, huh?" Faith said, emphasizing to herself what this man was capable of. "I take it you're not gonna tell me your name. Can you at least give me a fake one?"

"You can call me Doyle."

"Well thanks for fucking my day up even more than it already was, Doyle."

"You ain't gettin' no sympathy from me, so don't bark up that tree. If you were a law-abidin' citizen, you wouldn't have been at Paul Wilcox's house and I wouldn't have caught you with illegal shit. If it makes ya feel better, think of yourself as a martyr. A few hours of agony for a noble cause. Bet it's the most noble thing you've done in a long time and I'm givin' ya that chance. You're very welcome."

Before Faith could point out the ridiculousness of his statement, Doyle announced excitedly, "There he is!" He quickly got out of the car and opened her door.

"What are we doing?" she asked, dumbfounded.

"We're walkin'. I can't have anyone seein' this car at the bar. Come on, get out."

They walked a quarter mile or so in silence. The situation she found herself in made Faith want to cry. She could feel the tears building up, but a solid wall of disbelief kept them at bay. She was seriously considering the idea that she was sleeping. She checked the time on her watch, then looked away. A few seconds later she checked it again. It was the same, she was awake.

She gave herself a pep talk in her head to distract herself from how badly she was shaking. She reassured herself that it would be a walk in the park.

Go in, wait a while, work up tears, call the police, make up a story … a story. What do I say?

"What am I supposed to tell the cops?"

"Whatever you want. Tell them you met some guy and decided to go there to fool around. Things escalated too quickly, you said no but started feeling woozy. Then you woke up with your pants off."

"But won't they give me an examination? They'll know I'm lying."

"Just refuse it. Often in cases like this, the victim is too traumatized and sensitive to agree to an exam. No one will make you, though they'll try like hell to convince you."

Faith felt her phone vibrating in her pocket. She hadn't thought about it since being pulled over, but was glad to realize now that it wasn't left in her pocketbook back in the car. She peeked at the screen inconspicuously. It was Jake. The craziness of the past half hour made her forget all about him. He was probably still reeling from her message earlier. He would still think she was planning to kill herself. Or worse, that she already did. She needed to tell him what was going on, but knew answering the phone would make Doyle snatch it away.

Then she had a thought. There was a way out of this mess. She didn't need to go through with his plan. Doyle fucked himself and she could use it to her advantage. If she could notify Jake that she was in trouble, he would come to the bar and the ruckus caused by his arrival and confrontation of Doyle would catch the attention of everyone in it. Doyle wouldn't be able to reveal himself as a cop and would be forced to leave her alone, since she would have the protection of Jake and the bar's occupants. She would be free to go to the police and report him. Sure, Doyle wasn't his real name, but it wouldn't be hard to identify him using other means. He would be cornered. She wouldn't even have to worry about the drugs and the gun, since they were out of her car, had no connection to her, and Doyle's word wouldn't mean shit at that point.

He was truly a dumb bastard. Faith had to suppress a smile. The phone stopped ringing and Jake left a message. She couldn't check it, but she was sure she could text him without taking the phone out of the pocket of her sweatshirt.

After a few minutes of fumbling and hiding her messaging from Doyle, she managed to text what she hoped was: "Can't talk or listen to voicemail you left. In trouble. Go to Husky Harry's. Please come. In Rain Room." Jake knew what Husky Harry's was. They made fun of the place plenty of times together. He'd never been there, but once he arrived, he would find the Rain Room easily enough.

They arrived at the bar at last. "It's go time," Doyle said, stopping in front of the door and turning to her. "Don't do any talkin', I'll take care of everything. Just do as I say." He opened the door and motioned for her to enter first. She did. The bar was almost completely empty. Only three people sat drinking.

The two approached the counter and Doyle leaned on it to get the bartender's attention. "Excuse me sir, could you point me in the direction of the owner please?"

The bartender, an attractive Latino man, responded, "He got here just a minute ago. He's in the back office, I'll grab him for you." His name tag identified him as Jorge.

"Good man," Doyle said, then grabbed Faith by the waist and guided her onto a stool.

"Can I get you two something while you wait?" Jorge asked.

"I'll take a CC and Seven. What do you want, Faith?"

"I'm good," she responded. She was actually parched, but hoped Jorge would notice something was off if she acted melancholic.

"Get her a water," Doyle told him. She was relieved that she got the drink anyway.

"Sure thing."

A door opened at the far end of the bar, past two rows of pool tables. A man appeared from behind it.

"There he is now, sir," Jorge said, pointing toward him.

Doyle looked Faith in the eyes sternly and whispered, "Stay here. Don't think about leaving. I'll take you down to the station or worse if you try anything dumb."

Faith shrugged off his threat as he walked to the owner, Phil. He didn't look like a bad guy to her, but then again, there were plenty of charismatic criminals. The bartender put their drinks in front of her and she nodded in thanks.

She hadn't had a chance to realize how exhausted she was. The fact struck her now as she rested her head in her hands and closed her eyes. She would have given anything for some sleep. A voice interrupted her peace.

"Name's Amy, hun. What's yours?" It was soft-spoken, but still startled her. She snapped her head up and saw a very dark girl, younger than she was. She appeared to Faith to be either crazy or high. Despite her calm demeanor, she had an intense look in her eyes. Her hair didn't look like it had been combed for a long while and the purple tank-top she wore was loose and worn out.

Huh?" Faith asked, then caught the question before the so-called Amy was forced to repeat herself. "Oh … uh, Faith. My name's Faith." She wasn't up for small talk. She was tired and her body was beginning to ask for more heroin.

"Lovely name. Now Faith, I couldn't help but notice you seem to be in an awfully unpleasant situation with your man-friend over there." Faith was already stressed from her situation, the lack of drugs and her weariness. An unhinged stranger overstepping her boundaries was just added trouble.

"He's not my friend – and keep out of my business."

"I only mention it because if that's a bad man you got yourself tangled up with, I can help you out. I happen to know someone who doesn't take kindly to men who treat women badly."

Faith was about to tell her to screw off, but before she had the chance to, the girl did it to herself, albeit in a new, deeper tone.

"Fuck that, you cretinous shrew, I'm not helping anyone." The voice was directly out of a horror movie. Faith's suspicions about the girl's sanity were confirmed and she was now genuinely fearful of her. She didn't know how to react and was surprised to find herself wishing Doyle was there.

"I, uh …" she began, but couldn't find appropriate words. Amy continued, talking more to herself than to Faith.

"Not that I'd help such a piss-poor example of a woman anyhow. She's a worm who will do anything for a fix. Just look at her arms." Faith wished she had a sweatshirt on.

The crazy bitch now aimed her verbal assault directly at Faith. "Scum. I bet you'd sell your own kid to get high for five minutes. People like you contribute nothing to this world and bring the rest of humanity down. You just take and take, then wallow in your own pettiness, wearing it like a fucking badge."

Faith's fear transformed into rage. "You have no fucking clue who I am or how I live."

"I know exactly how you live. Like a fucking rat! I bet that scar you carry is drug-related. Just another souvenir of your lifestyle, along with your track marks. Your entire being reeks of trash."

The mention of her scar hit Faith hard, even more so than being called out for her marked arms. She reverted to her earlier state of mind, wishing she could leave the world for good. She desperately wanted to be with Jake, away from this bizarre reality she found herself in.

"You're fucking crazy, you psycho bitch. And you don't look like a fucking prize yourself. Talking like you're contributing shit to this world. Look at you, with your ragged clothes and ratty hair. You look like a damn hook—" she was stopped mid-sentence by Doyle.

"What's all the fuss about, Faith?" he asked. She was glad to see him, even though she knew he was rescuing her from one hell and dragging her to another. "And who the fuck is this?"

"It's no one. Are we doing this or what?" She got up, eager to get far away from the psychopath.

"Right this way, firecracker," Doyle said, then grabbed both of their drinks. Faith hoped Jake had gotten her message and was on his way. She didn't know how long Doyle would stay in the room with her, but it had to be long enough to make a rape seem plausible.

She walked toward a door at the back of the bar with a sign above it that read, "The Rain Room." The sight of the room and the thought of what it was used for disgusted her. Something in her wanted to go through with Doyle's plan, just to see it shut down. But she couldn't risk being involved in a fraud like that, even if it *did* put that fucker away. It wasn't so much the ethical quandary that bothered her, but the possibility of getting in serious legal trouble for some douchebag who had beaten her within minutes of them meeting.

The two entered the room, which was surprisingly clean.

The walls were painted a light blue, which was possibly the origin of the name. It was a welcomed change from the wood-paneling that lined the rest of the establishment. There was a couch – which Faith was wary of touching – and a side table with a phone on it. A flat-screen television hung on the wall, presumably in case anyone was in there for any reason other than to screw.

"Sit down," Doyle commanded. She did as she was told. "Now go ahead and repeat the plan to me."

She grabbed her water, took a large sip and cleared her throat. "In a little bit, you're gonna leave. I'm gonna wait a while and then I'm gonna go out and say I was drugged and raped. Once the police are here, I tell them that I saw the owner give you a pill before we came in the room."

"And when they ask how you met me?"

"I'll tell them I met you outside and we decided to hang out in here. I thought we were just gonna make out or something."

"Not very creative, but it'll do the job. There's one thing I didn't tell you before that I should now. When you leave this room, you need to look like you've been drugged."

"Well I guess I can do my best at acting like it." She hoped her plan would come together so she wouldn't have to.

He paused a moment and said, "You won't have to. You just ingested GHB."

She dropped her glass of water, breaking it into shards that scattered about the room. She desperately jammed her finger down her throat in an attempt to throw the drug up. She knew it wouldn't work, she was never able to make herself vomit.

"Don't bother, you're only gonna hurt yourself," he said calmly. "Sit on the couch and relax. You'll be fine in a bit, and the whole thing will be over."

She was suddenly desperate to escape the room. If he drugged her, what was stopping him from making the setup even more realistic? Would she even know if he did?

She stood up. "I have to use the bathroom," she said in a feeble attempt at getting free.

"Too bad, sit the fuck down." She did. Her foot brushed a large piece from her destroyed glass. She feared that the sharp edge was her only key out of the situation, unless Jake showed up very soon. She didn't know if she could bring herself to kill anyone, let alone a cop. That's if he even truly was one. She decided it didn't matter, it was about survival now. It was self defense. That warranted any means necessary.

"Just give it a few minutes and you'll feel loopy," Doyle said, as if he were talking casually about how his day was. "I'll wait a little bit and take off. No harm will come to you, I promise." It was a lie, she knew it. He was going to take advantage of her once the drugs hit.

Doyle sighed heavily. "Good intentions brought me to this, whether you believe that or not. Bad people should be handled swiftly, efficiently. Instead, they're coddled and given the benefit of the doubt even when there's no doubt to be had. It sickens me."

He paced as he spoke, not paying much attention to Faith. She found an opening and grabbed the large shard from the floor. He turned to her a second after she buried it in the cushion.

"You work this job for as long as I have, you start to think of ways to circumvent the legal system. You pull over a fuckin' nigger or spic with some drugs on him and you think, 'A bullet to the brain would take care of this trash so much faster than an arrest.' Now, whether you do it or not depends on the kind of person y'are. But these thoughts overwhelm you until you can't help but take action."

Faith dug out the glass dagger from the couch and stood up quietly while Doyle faced the other way. She crept toward him as he continued to speak.

"Jeremy Bentham said 'It is the greatest good to the greatest number of people which is the measure of right and wrong.' So if I gotta bend the rules and hurt a junkie or two in the process, then I guess—" Faith looked past his shoulder to the television that hung on the wall. It was off, the black picture showing a reflection of the room. With her weapon raised, their eyes met in the screen.

Doyle spun around in an instant and fired Paul's pistol from his waist. The shot pushed Faith back, and after keeping her balance for a second, she dropped to the ground. She didn't know where she was hit. Her entire body was in pain and the shock was too great to allow her to search for the wound. She closed her eyes and waited. Whether she was waiting for death or salvation, she didn't know. Didn't care. The only thing she could coherently hope for in that moment was to see Jake's face.

When she opened her eyes, her wish was reality.

She didn't know how, but she was now lying in Jake's lap, his worried face gazing down at her. The sight made her the happiest she'd ever been. If this was the end, his face would be burned in her soul for eternity. What more could she ask for?

"Oh God, Faith," he said desperately. "No, no, no." There was a lot of movement but she didn't know what he was doing. Then he yelled, "Someone call 9-1-1! Please, for Christ's sake, call 9-1-1! Anyone!" His panic-stricken voice made her worry for him. Death was here to claim her, and Jake knew it. He lowered his head onto hers and she could feel his tears run down her face. She held his arm.

"You're gonna be OK, you hear me?" he tried to reassure her. "This is nothing." She wasn't buying it. She shook her head, hoping he would find solace in her serenity.

She had to get a last message out to him. He had to know how she felt.

"I'm ... I'm so sorry," she whispered. "I'm sorry I was a burden. Thank you for ... thank you for loving me anyway."

The end was closing in. She wanted to say how grateful she was that he never left her alone. How he made the pitiful life she had worth living. That without him she wouldn't have lasted as long as she did. She hoped he knew how much he mattered to her, how he was the most important thing in her life.

Her dying body wouldn't let her say all that.

"You ..." She couldn't force the words out, didn't have the strength. As darkness washed over her, she prayed that he could hear her thoughts.

You made sure I wasn't empty in the end.

Entry from
Detective Arthur Candle's Journal
Dated: October 17, 2008

Well, I finally did it. I finally took my therapist's advice and decided to write in this damn journal that's been sitting on my bookshelf for 2 months. That's when you know something's really fucked up. When Arthur Candle writes in a fucking journal. Apparently it took a bunch of dead people to put my mind in the place it needed to be to grab a pen and get this shit out of me.

I don't even know what I'm supposed to write. My feelings? How my day was? I don't have any and it sucked.

Got called to a tough one tonight. Wasn't ready for it. Worst crime scene I've ever been misfortunate enough to walk into. Got there and was told 7 people were dead. Fucking shit, Journal. I've investigated scenes with 7 bodies before, don't get me wrong. But homicides like that are always gang-related, so they don't weigh too heavy on my mind. This was different. This was regular people, damnit. For the most part, anyway. Slaughtered. It was disgusting.

The causes of death were all over the place. The targets were all over the place, literally and figuratively. I don't think I'll ever know how it all came together. I've already learned a lot, though.

This was the worst possible time for this shit. Fucking depression's at an all-time high. Or low, I guess, depending on how you look at it. I feel blank. I *am* blank. I feel the exact same emotion with loved ones as I do when I'm shaving. Which is the same exact emotion I feel when I'm driving. The same as when I'm at a ball game. It's all the same. Crummy and low. I don't even know the meaning of fun anymore. It feels like some mythical, poetic concept that doesn't exist in the real world. Not my version of it, at least. Whatever fun is, it's been erased from my system.

Fixing this shit doesn't even entice me. It'd be like throwing a piece of myself away. Scares me more than any fucking criminal. There's a strange intimacy to feeling like this. Living in your head so damn much, apart from the outside world. It's an intimacy with yourself, who you hate, but love to hate.

What am I even fucking talking about? Sitting here feeling pity for myself, rambling. Fuck it, it's my goddamn journal. I can write about whatever the fuck I want. Wish I had some scotch.

I don't even know why I get out of bed in the morning. I never have to wonder what the day will bring. It's bringing the same bullshit as always. Dead bodies. Bosses breathing down my neck. Self-hatred. The fuck is the point? Wish someone would just take me out already.

I never realized before how much of a nihilist I am.

It ain't all bad, though, despite how much I bitch and whine. Something extraordinary happened at that crime scene tonight. Something that gave me a dull inkling of happiness.

I'm looking at all the bodies, taking notes, gathering facts. I usually get an overview of the victims, then go back for a closer look once I've taken the whole scene in. One of them's an 11-year-old kid. Looked just like my nephew Robbie. He was face-down on the concrete. Fucking bullet in the back of his head. I almost cried, I swear. Hey, there's emotion in me after all!

Then I see movement. His back elevates a tiny bit. The little trooper was breathing. I called for a paramedic.

I sat with him in the ambulance. He cracked his eyes open and I told him, "You're gonna be alright, son. You're gonna be alright." Don't know if I actually believed it, but he needed to hear me say it. Doctors said he was gonna be fine. He was responsive in no time. Fucking fighter, that boy. Gotta remember to check in with him in a day or two.

Don't know if I'd make it through a shot to the head like he did. Don't know if I'd want to.

I questioned him briefly on his way into the operating room. I learned a couple things. Not much. Enough. Enough to do what needed to be done.

My therapist is full of shit. This didn't help at all.

Doyle's Guilt

Officer Casey O'Doyle fumbled with his keys, struggling to stop his fingers from shaking long enough to unlock the door. The hall was dark, which only added to his feeling of dread and paranoia. He looked behind him. No one was there. The key finally slid into the old lock and he opened the door to his apartment.

He flipped the light switch in the kitchen, opened the fridge and grabbed a beer, hoping it would calm his nerves. He was a wreck. Life as he knew it could be snatched away from him at any second. Too much had happened for him to cover his tracks completely, but he had done the best he could. There was nothing left to do but wait and hope.

He was sure to grab his credit card and ID from behind the bar counter when he arrived back at Husky Harry's in full uniform. It was a surprise to him when Phil Harris asked for them; he was caught off guard. Luckily he was in a position to get them back before any of the other officers found them. He'd arrived back to his squad car from the bloodbath just in time to get the call on the radio. A minute later he was dressed for the job and on his way back to the bar.

Detective Candle interviewed the bartender. It was a damn good thing, too, because Jorge would have identified O'Doyle in a heartbeat. No one else in the bar had gotten a good look at him. No one still alive, at least. Candle was the lead detective in the case so it was crucial to stay out of his way and off his radar. O'Doyle didn't think he suspected anything, didn't think he had any reason to. The future was a mystery, though. There might have been traces of his DNA in Husky Harry's, but he didn't think he ever took a sip of his CC and Seven. He hoped he didn't. Candle didn't seem like he brought his A-game that night, anyway. He was fatigued when they spoke earlier.

"I've seen a whole lot over the years," Candle said inside Husky Harry's, "but good God, this one's fucked." He had circles around his eyes so dark it looked like make-up.

"This city and the scum in it never cease to amaze me, boss," O'Doyle responded. He didn't need to try to sound surprised at the scene. To his shock, there were two more bodies than he'd left there.

"But why do they do it?" Candle asked rhetorically. "What's so hard about living an honest life, just going about your business without acting like a menace. Look at this place. It's right out of a friggin' movie. What kind of beast did all this?"

O'Doyle itched his nose. "My guess is it's drug-related. Probably started as a petty dispute and erupted from there. You know how this area is. Damn shame."

"Fucking right, it is." Candle rubbed his eyes and sighed. "Don't know how much longer I can go on seeing this shit. I need to catch this one. I need a win, for Christ's sake."

In the two hours before returning home, O'Doyle had completely cleaned out his car, getting rid of any evidence that that fucking bitch was ever there.

She just couldn't stick to the fuckin' plan, he thought, livid. *Phil should be in a cell right now. Instead, I'm on the fuckin' run because of a freak fuckin' slaughter that should've never fuckin' happened. Fuck.*

The whole thing was surreal. One minute his plan was going perfectly, and the next he'd killed four people. As if his situation wasn't bad enough after shooting Faith, that psycho nigger bitch just came out of nowhere and fucked things up even more for him. He didn't want Phil dead, just punished, rotting away in a concrete room. Even so, he wasn't all that torn up about his death.

For the first time that O'Doyle could remember, he was afraid. A picture of himself in a jail cell flashed in his mind. The whole situation was too much of a clusterfuck. There had to be something leading back to him. There were witnesses. There were bullets. There were connections. His mind zipped through every detail. Every bullet shot, every doorknob touched, every word spoken, every breath taken.

The gun he used had no connections to him, he was confident in that. He wiped it clean and ditched it in a dumpster miles away, along with Faith's dope and the clothes he was wearing. God knows how much those drugs were worth. It took a whole lot of discipline to trash them. In the end, his freedom was worth more than the risk.

He emptied the beer bottle with a large gulp and tossed it in the sink. The shine of the glass made his nerves twitch. He'd be dead if he didn't look up at the television screen at that exact second. *Death by glass*, he thought, *that would have been a fuckin' bitch*.

He turned on the light in his living room, then jumped at

the sudden sound of a voice.

"Interesting scene out there tonight, huh Casey? Oh, I'm sorry … I mean, *Doyle*." It was Arthur Candle. He sat in the recliner with a beer in one hand and a pistol in the other, aiming it in O'Doyle's direction. "Now, let's skip the whole denial phase of this conversation," he continued, "because we both know damn well that you're guilty. Of what, I'm not so sure. Your handy work was far too fucked up for me to put all the pieces into place just now. I was hoping you'd do me the favor of explaining it to me."

O'Doyle didn't bother fighting it. Candle clearly knew for sure; he wasn't going to be persuaded otherwise.

"How'd you know? What did I forget to clean up?"

Candle took a swig of his drink. "One of the victims survived, Casey. Told me what he saw. Doesn't seem like you tried too hard to disguise yourself. Then again, I suppose you weren't planning on sparking a massacre when you woke up this morning, were you?"

"Who? Who survived?" O'Doyle's voice cracked as he asked the question.

"An eleven-year-old boy that you shot in the head as he ran away from you. His name was Gabriel Morrison."

"Oh, thank God for—"

"Stop. Just stop. Don't act like you're glad that there's a living witness. The bullet in his skull did plenty of damage, but it didn't kill him. What it *did* do, however, was put him to sleep. Turns out he's a narcoleptic. I know, right? Extreme circumstances cause him to pass out. What's more extreme than a bullet in the head, huh? I suspect someone will be fired for not realizing right away that he was still alive, despite his shallow breathing. Apparently I was the first son-of-a-bitch to check for a pulse.

"The kid said he saw you shoot the woman in the alley. Said Phil called you 'Doyle,' and that you were wearing an orange shirt with a motorcycle on it. C'mon, Casey. Really? You change your name from O'Doyle to Doyle, wear a shirt that even *I've* seen you in and expect to get away with murder?"

"I wasn't planning a murder," O'Doyle said, knowing it didn't matter for anything except to retain the little conscience he had left.

"Well what the fuck *were* you planning?"

"I wanted to put that fucker, Phil Harris away! It should have worked, but–"

"The owner? What the fuck did he ..." Candle stopped and thought for a second. "Is this about that girl that got raped a few months back? He had nothing to do with it. He wasn't even charged!" Candle scolded him like a disappointed parent.

"That was my fuckin' niece that got raped!" O'Doyle screamed, pointing his finger at Candle. "And just 'cause that motherfucker walked don't mean he wasn't guilty."

"I personally handled his interrogation, Casey. There wasn't even the tiniest shred of evidence against the guy, he was out of there in minutes. You're telling me you murdered six people on a misinformed fucking hunch? You stupid piece of shit."

"Phil was guilty!" O'Doyle was in tears now. The weight of the situation and his helplessness conquered him. "Tricia fuckin' told me so, fuck you and your evidence. And I didn't kill no six people. That little nigger cunt sliced Phil's throat right in front of me, and I have no idea what happened to the lady in the alley or the Driscoll kid.

"I didn't mean for anyone to die, Candle, I fuckin' swear it. I was gonna frame the guy. Then that fuckin' heroin addict tries to stab me and the next thing I know I'm on the run for murder. It was a freak fuckin' event."

"A freak fucking event that your ignorance set off," Candle shot back.

"Y'know what? I don't even give a flying fuck," O'Doyle said with tears still streaming down his face. He didn't care anymore, he knew his life was over. He decided to stand behind his actions and lay in the bed he made. "Because of me, there's a pimp, a junkie, a psycho and a sleazy fuck off the street."

"There's good, honest people dead. Not to mention a little boy in a fucking hospital bed. How can you be so twisted?"

"I'm broken! Is that what you wanna hear, you cocksucker? And y'know what broke me? This fuckin' job, Candle. This fuckin' piece of shit job that throws one loss after another in your fuckin' direction 'til you can't swat 'em away anymore. I feel like I've seen more dead bodies than live ones. I remember 'em all. Cops preach justice. There ain't no fuckin' justice and you know it. For every ten killers and rapists and thieves and drug dealers walking the street, we catch one. Is there any job on the planet that's as inefficient as that?"

"I don't give a fuck if we catch one in a hundred, I've got morals. I don't go around shooting up a bar full of people just because I don't like my fucking job! You know what it's like to hold a kid with a bullet hole in his head and tell him everything's gonna be alright? You fucking animal!"

"Oh, shove your morals up your fuckin' ass. Morals are for Christian fuckin' housewives. When did having morals ever help us put away a criminal, huh? You're soft, Candle. Y'know what I'd do right now if I were in your position? I'd put a bullet right between my fuckin' eyes. But you won't do that. No. Instead you're gonna cuff me, take me in, put me through the system.

"And for what? Maybe in a couple years I'll finally be behind bars, living off the taxpayer's dime. Might even get paroled somewhere down the line. No sir, I wouldn't go through all that trouble if I were you. I'd just empty the clip and end it here. Go ahead, you fuck. I ain't afraid of dyin'. There ain't no Hell waitin' for me. Just sleep – and I need it, trust me." He didn't know whether or not he wanted Candle to follow his advice, but it was honest, nonetheless.

Candle took down the rest of the beer and stood up. "Get on your knees, Casey." He stood with the gun in his hand, only his silhouette visible against the light from a street lamp streaming in through the window.

"You tryin' to scare me?" O'Doyle said with a giggle. "Fine, I'll play along. Here, I'm gettin' down." He knelt and put his hands behind his head mockingly. "You want some last words, too? How 'bout this: Fuck you. Fuck Phil Harris. Fuck Jacob Driscoll. Fuck Faith whatever-the-fuck-her-name-is. Fuck that psycho coon. Fuck Ron Toomey. Fuck that Miranda bitch. Fuck the kid, I hope he fuckin' dies. Fuck the worthless police department, with their heads so far up their fuckin' asses that they're feedin' themselves with their own shit. Fuck this city and the fuckin' Orange District. Fuck my life. Fuck this apartment, with its cracks, mold, chipped paint, broken switches, rats and drafty fuckin' windows. Fuck my whore mother. Fuck the sperm donor who fucked her and left me to be tormented by her. Fuck my acid reflux. Fuck all the cunts that think they're too fuckin' good to let me buy 'em a fuckin' drink. Fuck me for giving a flyin' fuck about any of it. Fuck you. Fuck the fact that I already said 'Fuck you.' I'll say it again. Fuck you!

"We both know you ain't gonna shoot me, Candle. You're

a punk pussy who can't handle the darker side of life; can't handle doin' what needs to be done. Plus, they'd trace the bullets from your gun back to you faster than you could say, 'I take dicks in the ass.'"

Candle walked behind him and leaned down, whispering in is ear, "I got this gun from your dresser drawer."

About the Author

Robert Sadler is an author, graphic designer and fine artist living in Massachusetts with his perfect someone. His favorite things are: great stories, art in any medium, peanut butter, books, music, orange (the color, not the fruit – though the fruit isn't half bad), challenges, coffee and anyone who has appreciated this book or any of his other creations. Oh, and writing lighthearted 'About the Author' blurbs to top off very serious novels.

www.ingramcontent.com/pod-product-compliance
Lightning Source LLC
Chambersburg PA
CBHW070817120626
46556CB00002B/541